Let's Begin Again

USA TODAY BESTSELLING AUTHOR

Heather B. Moore

Let's Begin Again

A PINE VALLEY NOVEL

Copyright © 2019 by Mirror Press, LLC
Print edition
All rights reserved

No part of this book may be reproduced in any form whatsoever without prior written permission of the publisher, except in the case of brief passages embodied in critical reviews and articles. This is a work of fiction. The characters, names, incidents, places, and dialogue are products of the author's imagination and are not to be construed as real.

Interior design by Cora Johnson
Edited by Kelsey Down and Lisa Shepherd
Cover design by Rachael Anderson
Cover image credit: Deposit Photos #35255315 by Alberto Bogo
Published by Mirror Press, LLC
ISBN-13: 978-1-947152-56-4

PINE VALLEY SERIES

Worth the Risk
Where I Belong
Say You Love Me
Waiting for You
Finding Us
Until We Kissed
Let's Begin Again

Let's Begin Again

When Maurie Ledbetter moves back to her hometown to open her dream shop, she calls a local construction crew for help. Former teenage crush Grant Shelton shows up on her front porch, answering the call for the construction job. Seeing Grant again brings back Maurie's memories of her troubled childhood, and she doesn't know if spending time around Grant is the best way to move on. But when she discovers Grant has gone through difficulties of his own, Maurie realizes that he might be the key to her own healing.

One

"Thank you, Mr. Finch." Maurie Ledbetter pressed END on her cell phone and collapsed onto the ratty floral couch. In two weeks, she'd be the new owner of the shop on the corner of Main Street in Pine Valley. She could hardly believe this was finally happening. Fourteen days. 336 hours—but who was counting?

Maurie dialed the number at the top of her contacts list, calling her best friend and one and only employee, Taffy.

"What's new?" Taffy answered, not one to stall with chitchat.

"We got it!" Maurie said. "We're about to open the bricks-and-mortar version of Every Occasion."

Taffy hooted, and Maurie laughed. Her heart seemed to be beating a mile a minute as the news finally sunk in.

"When do you close on the property?" Taffy asked.

Maurie rose from the couch and walked around the boxes strewn about the living room, her mind reeling with all the to-dos. "Two weeks. The realtor said it was unusual to have such a quick closing period, but the seller agreed."

"Wow," Taffy said. "Who would have thought two years ago that your little online hobby of selling gift baskets would turn into this?"

"I know, right?" Maurie peered out of the newly scrubbed living-room window. The neighborhood beyond was the same quiet neighborhood of her childhood. "When are you coming? We need to get the signs ordered and decide on a grand opening date and print off a million fliers—"

"Whoa," Taffy cut in with her bubbly laugh that seemed to complement her curly blonde hair and energetic personality. "Last I googled, Pine Valley only has twelve hundred residents. And even with the tourist ski crowd, our customer base wouldn't come close to a *million*."

Maurie released a breath. "You're right. I'm just up to my armpits in boxes, and I need to make a list of stuff to do now that the offer on the shop was accepted."

Outside, two little girls rode along the cracked sidewalk, one on a red bike, the other on a blue one. They were laughing at something, and Maurie's stomach pinched. She'd once been a carefree kid like those girls, but that was before . . . Well, the past was going to stay in the past, where it was meant to be. And the next step in Maurie's plan was renovating this dumpy house of her mother's. As soon as things at the shop were organized, Maurie would start with ripping out the carpets, then move on to burning all the furniture and—

"Hello?" Taffy said. "Are you still there?"

"Oh, sorry." Maurie exhaled. "I'm already making more lists. You know me. When are you coming?"

"I just told you," Taffy said, indulgent laughter in her voice. "I'm packing tonight and leaving first thing in the morning. Should make Pine Valley by dinner."

Maurie turned from the window and the young, innocent, laughing girls. "Perfect. I'll wash the new guest-bedroom sheets I bought, and I might even venture to the grocery store before you get here."

"I can grab McDonald's on the way into town," Taffy said. "Want a cheeseburger and fries?"

"Don't you dare," Maurie said. "That stuff tastes like grease and bad memories."

"Doesn't bother me," Taffy quipped.

"Seriously," Maurie said. "I'll have dinner ready when you get here. I'd like to try a new chicken-salad recipe I found on Pinterest."

Taffy gave a good-natured sigh. "You're a nut, you know that? I mean, don't you have enough to do? Cooking should be at the *bottom* of the list."

"That's why *you're* coming to work for me," Maurie reminded her. "To keep my priorities straight." She eyed the boxes and a stack of wicker baskets.

"All right, Boss," Taffy said. "See you tomorrow."

Maurie was smiling when she hung up the phone. She pressed the phone against her chest and turned back to the window. She'd done it. She had returned to the hometown that she'd left ten years ago at the age of seventeen, moved into the house she'd inherited from the mother who'd disowned her, and now would be an official shop owner in Pine Valley.

She crossed to the tiny kitchen area, fired up the laptop she'd left on the counter, then googled *handyman in Pine Valley*. Several hits popped up—all in Pine Valley, Utah. Maurie refined her search to *California*. A couple of construction companies and their websites popped up. There were quite a few luxury cabins in the area, near the slopes, belonging to the who's who crowd. These construction companies certainly catered to the wealthy, if their ten-thousand-square-foot cabins were any indication.

She hovered over one link and read aloud, "Briggs Brothers. Your hometown handymen. No job is too small."

She clicked and opened the simple website. In the top left corner was a picture of two men. Both men wore baseball caps, shading their faces, so Maurie couldn't see either of them clearly. Not that she knew a lot of people in Pine Valley anymore. And she certainly didn't remember the name of Briggs.

Her mom had homeschooled her since middle school, insisting that the public system was failing her child—a notion which Maurie had allowed herself to believe for a long time. It wasn't until she was removed from the home—after a raucous party her mother had thrown and was subsequently busted for—and placed in another city in foster care, that Maurie discovered she was academically nearly two years behind her peers. Maurie was never returned home because her mother had gone to jail for six months for possession of illegal substances and endangering a minor. And when she was released, she'd written a letter to Maurie saying she was relinquishing parental rights to the state.

Now, ten years later, the memory of the letter still stung, although it had long ago been destroyed. Fortunately, Maurie had landed in a decent foster home, and her foster mom, Gladys Ronning, had shown her what a real mother's love could be like.

Thinking of Gladys still made Maurie emotional. Gladys hadn't been perfect, but she'd been the best mom Maurie had ever had. Because of Gladys, Maurie had pulled her life together and discovered she could set and keep goals.

Maurie wiped a tear off her cheek and took a deep breath as she stared, unseeing, at the Briggs Brothers website. Gladys had died when Maurie was in college. A year later, Maurie had been notified by the state that her mother had died as well. Causes unknown. It had been several more months before

Maurie was contacted by a Pine Valley lawyer about her mother's estate. After hanging up from the phone call, Maurie had laughed at the news, and then she'd cried. Later, she'd called the lawyer back and told him to rent the house out. At the time she was still in college and wasn't ready to change her life all over again and move back to her past.

That had all changed a couple of months ago, when Mr. Right had turned out to be Mr. Completely Wrong, and Maurie needed to start her life over . . . miles and miles away from Irvine, where she'd been living. Miles away from Brandon.

Pine Valley had suddenly seemed a safe haven.

"Well, I'm here now," Maurie said aloud to the empty kitchen. "And I'm about ready to be a store owner."

Since the house had been paid off long ago by Maurie's grandparents before her mother inherited it, the years of rent, minus upkeep expenses, had been accumulating in an account. Eventually, it had added up to a sizable down payment for Maurie's new beginning.

She took a deep breath and dialed the number for Briggs Brothers. A woman answered—a secretary, it seemed. She took down Maurie's address, then promised someone would be out that afternoon to evaluate her needs and work up a bid.

"*This* afternoon? That's quick," Maurie said.

"It *is* January, ma'am," the woman said in a brisk tone. "Not much construction going on in Pine Valley this time of year."

"Okay, that makes sense." Maurie felt chagrined and annoyed at the same time, for being called *ma'am*. She was only twenty-seven. But the woman on the other end of the line had no way of knowing that. "Great, and thank you so much," Maurie said.

When she hung up, she stood and stretched, then

grabbed her notebook of lists and more lists. She turned to a fresh page and started planning for a visit from Briggs Brothers.

Two

Grant Shelton stared at the address of the work order on his phone. Then he looked over at the dilapidated house, with its overgrown, dead lawn mostly covered in snow. At least the walkway had been shoveled clear of the recent snowfall. His gaze cut to the house number stenciled on its mailbox. *Yep.* It was the right place. He groaned.

Switching to his phone's contacts, he called Julie. When his sister answered, he said, "Who called you from 462 Elmwood?"

"Uh, hang on." It sounded like she was typing something on her keyboard. "Let's see . . . Maurie Ledbetter."

Grant clenched his jaw. It took him a moment to re-focus his thoughts. "Hey, this might sound really weird, but do you think Dave could do this bid?"

Julie laughed. "Grant, you're funny. Yesterday over dinner you told my husband that you needed more hours. Ask and ye shall receive, hon."

Grant rubbed a hand down his face. He did need the extra income. His stupid legal battle with Joy was driving him crazy and draining his meager savings. "Yeah, you're right, Julie."

If ever a name was an oxymoron, it was his ex-wife's. And now Joy had revised their custody agreement so she could keep their four-year-old son, Trent, with her full-time, limiting Grant's visits to little more than holidays and summers... Because *she'd* moved a hundred miles south with her new boyfriend, Stone. Yep. That was his name. *Stone.*

"Grant, you okay?" Julie's voice sounded with genuine concern.

"Sorry about that," Grant said. "I'm not thinking straight."

"You're going through a tough time." His sister's tone was tender, which only made him feel worse for balking at this job. "Keep your chin up, and remember to enjoy the work. You're an amazing carpenter, and not many people get to follow their passion."

His sister was right. "I know," he said. "It's been one of those weeks, I guess."

After Julie married Dave Briggs, Grant had thought a partnership was the perfect solution to his problems. For years he'd been trying to make it solo as a carpenter, but he hadn't been able to compete for bigger contracts against the elite construction companies in the area. Together he and Dave had carved out their own niche as hometown handymen, often cleaning up the bigger construction companies' mistakes. In between chasing her two kids around, Julie took care of their accounting and scheduling.

"Come over for dinner tonight," Julie continued. "You can't work a full day on a cup of coffee."

Julie knew him well. But today, Grant hadn't even had coffee that morning, and at the mention of food he realized how hungry he was. Usually he at least grabbed a sandwich from the Main Street Café on his way through town, but there'd been no time today. After hanging up with Julie, he climbed out of his work truck and headed up the icy drive. There was no point putting off this meeting any longer. With each step, all kinds of thoughts and emotions churned within him. He didn't know if he had enough fortitude to face his past with Maurie Ledbetter.

There was no chance that she wasn't *the* Maurie he'd known when they were teenagers. It had been ten years, yes, but Grant had never gotten over the guilt—the guilt he'd felt after calling the police that night, which had turned out to be Maurie's last night in Pine Valley with her mom.

When Grant had found out that Maurie had been taken into protective custody and put into foster care, he'd felt gutted. He had only wanted to protect her from her mother's deadbeat boyfriend. Everyone had known that Joe was bad news—Joe being Grant's mom's cousin, so Grant was privy to the details. And when Grant had seen Joe coming out of Maurie's home one evening, Grant's blood had frozen in his veins.

At the time, he'd assessed what he knew about Maurie— she was a couple of years younger than him, was homeschooled, and sat on her porch to watch the kids walk home after school. He lived down the street from her and had passed by her house often. Mrs. Ledbetter was a single mom who lived in her deceased parents' home. Grant had heard the talk around town about Mrs. Ledbetter's string of boyfriends, but Joe had been the worst yet of those bad-news guys.

Grant shook the memories from his mind as he climbed the front steps to the Ledbetter house. Once he rang that doorbell, there'd be no going back. He'd have to face the woman whose life he'd changed forever.

The door swung open while Grant was still gathering his courage.

"Oh, sorry," a female voice said, opening the screen door

as well. "I thought I saw the truck out front and wondered . . ." Her voice trailed off as she stared at him.

Grant couldn't stop staring back. The Maurie he remembered had been a thin, pale girl with a mop of black curls and round glasses hiding bright-green eyes.

This Maurie was the same person . . . but grown up and transformed. It was the only way to describe her. Her dark hair was still curly, but now it lay in soft waves skimming her shoulders. Her glasses were gone, and her eyes were just as green as ever. She was fair, yes, but not pale. In fact, her skin was more of a honey tone, as if she spent time outside. And she had a smattering of light freckles across her nose.

"Grant Shelton?" she said in a disbelieving half whisper.

He nodded. "Hi, Maurie." He held out his hand to dispel the awkwardness. How much did she remember of that night? Did she hate him for it?

She shook his hand, surprising him with a firm grip.

"It's been a long time," she continued, then released his hand.

It was all that Grant could do to nod again as he swallowed against his dry throat.

"Come in," she said. "I didn't mean to leave you standing on the porch in the cold."

She was normal. Totally normal. Friendly and . . . beautiful, if Grant was to be honest with himself. She was taller than he remembered, only about six inches shorter than him, and as he followed her inside, he had to drag his gaze away from her curves. She'd definitely grown up from that skinny girl he remembered.

They passed through a dim living room with wood paneling, a sagging couch, and boxes stacked everywhere. Grant followed Maurie into the kitchen. He had to force himself not to gawk. The kitchen was a disaster. Nothing had been updated in decades, and it looked as if Maurie had moved from one of those luxury resort cabins and crammed everything into this small house.

"Here." Maurie handed over a piece of paper. "My list of to-dos. Just so we're on the same page and so I don't repeat myself."

He wondered if she wore contacts, or if her eyes had always been this intense green. There was some brown in them too. So . . . hazel? He looked down at the paper she'd handed him. He tried to read the list, but his thoughts wouldn't compute. There were lists of words, all of them he should be able to read, but not one word made sense.

He glanced up at her, only to see she was studying him as well. Even though Pine Valley was in the dead of winter, this small house sure held its heat well. Maybe it had a newer furnace. Grant waited for Maurie to say something about their past. About the last time she'd lived in Pine Valley. How her mother's boyfriend had driven his car into the elm tree across the street. How her mother had thrown beer bottles at Joe from the front porch.

"I know there's a lot of little things on the list that might seem nitpicky," Maurie said, pulling Grant from his reverie. "But I'm opening a shop in town, so anything you can do here will free me up to focus more on my shop."

Grant's mind caught up with what she was saying. "What kind of shop?"

"Well . . ." she hedged. Then she smiled.

Grant tightened his grip on the paper he held. He felt that smile all the way to his feet.

"It's a gift shop called Every Occasion," Maurie said. "We specialize in gift baskets. I've been running it online for a couple of years now." She waved a hand at all the boxes and clutter. "Orders arrive daily, and I can't wait to move all of this to the shop. I close in thirteen and a half days."

Grant blinked. "Thirteen and a half, huh?"

Her cheeks pinked, and Grant couldn't decide what he liked more: her smile or her blush. Then he chastised himself for letting his mind wander to places it shouldn't. His life already had plenty of relationship baggage. And if Maurie thought Grant was attracted to her, after everything that had happened between them, she'd probably give him a well-deserved punch.

But here he was.

"I'll give you the grand tour," Maurie said with a smirk. "We're standing in the kitchen, of course. And once things get moved, you'll have plenty more room to work. As you can see, there's a lot of updating to do, and probably more than I realize."

"That's usually what happens with most jobs," Grant said. "But we'll keep the price as low as possible."

Maurie studied him for a second. "I'd appreciate that."

The air between them seemed to shift. "No problem."

Maurie turned. "Let's leave the kitchen for last. There's a giant hole in the wall in the hallway that needs to be patched."

Grant tried not to ogle Maurie as she led him through the house and pointed out the repairs. Everything she showed him were obvious surface repairs, and he could very well guess that once he started working, more and more things would be uncovered.

"Mind if I add a few things?" Grant said, taking a pen from his pocket and writing on the notepaper that Maurie had given him. He paused by the bathroom door in the hallway. "For instance, this doorframe is rotting and growing mold. And instead of replacing the door, the entire frame should be changed."

"That bad, huh?"

Grant gestured to the small window on the other side of

the bathroom. "Not much ventilation in here," he said. "But it looks like it was hit with something heavy, like a piece of furniture. See this splintering?"

Maurie said nothing for a moment, and when Grant met her gaze, she was frowning.

"If it's a matter of cost, I could start with the repairs that are most dire to make the place liveable," he said. "Then in a few months, move on to the others."

"That's not it," Maurie said. "I just remembered something, that's all." She flashed him a smile, but it wasn't like the genuine one earlier. "Yes, write down any additional repairs that you think are necessary. I want this place in good condition."

Grant wanted to question her more. Did she remember why this doorframe was cracked? Her life in this house must not have been too horrible, he decided, if she was willing to live here. It was a thought that made him feel even guiltier about his role in her becoming a foster kid.

"Do you want a total bid for everything on the list?" he asked as they moved into one of the bedrooms. He assumed it was where she was sleeping. It contained fewer boxes, and the bedding was rumpled but new. "Or do you prefer it itemized?"

"A total cost will be fine," Maurie said. "It all needs to be done, and I'd rather have it finished sooner than later." She pointed at the faded curtains on the window. "Do you install blinds too?"

"Sure," Grant said. "What about the carpets? It's not on your list, but they're pretty threadbare."

"You noticed that, did you?" Maurie's lips curved with amusement.

Grant wished he hadn't worn his sweatshirt. The bedroom was plenty warm, or maybe it was because it was the bedroom of this beautiful woman. Or because he didn't want her to think he was trying to get more money out of her. "One of my friends is a carpet layer."

"Who?" she asked.

"Shawn Anders. He was a couple of years older than me in school. Not sure if you knew him."

"Doesn't sound familiar."

She moved past him, close enough that he caught the scent of peppermint. Grant followed, and they inspected the second bedroom.

"This will be my friend Taffy's room for the time being," Maurie said. "She works for me and will help set up the shop. She doesn't want to move here permanently. But I'm planning on convincing her."

Grant took in the bare mattress and more stacked boxes. "Were you friends before you hired her, or the other way around?" For some reason, he wanted Maurie to have good friends.

"We were friends first," Maurie said. "When you meet her, you'll understand why I hired her. She has twice as much energy as anyone I know. She's also great with customers. Makes them feel like a million bucks even though they're not getting a full refund."

Grant leaned against the wall, watching Maurie talk. He couldn't remember her saying much when he knew her years ago. She'd always seemed so shy. But this Maurie didn't have a problem with conversation.

"What's your return policy?" He wasn't planning on buying a gift basket any time soon, or returning it for that matter, but he was drawn to watching Maurie talk about her business.

"Full refund in the first three days," Maurie said. "Otherwise, the customer only gets a percentage back. Some of the items are perishable, you know."

Grant nodded as if he understood, although he wasn't sure what went into her gift baskets.

Maurie pointed to the ceiling. "It would be great to have a fan in here," she said. "I remember this room as being hot and stuffy in the summers. Can you do electrical too?"

It was then that Grant realized this room must have been her childhood bedroom. "Yeah, I can install a fan."

Maurie's green eyes were back on him. "When did you learn all this stuff?"

A buzz warmed his skin at the appreciation in her eyes. "I always liked working with my hands. Worked construction summers in high school, and one thing led to another."

Maurie nodded. "Well, would you like a drink while you run the numbers?" She walked out of the room, which made it feel completely bare.

Grant followed, and again he had to concentrate to keep his gaze off the sway of her hips as she walked down the hall toward the kitchen.

Maybe he should date at least once in a while. Being around Maurie made him realize how much he'd isolated himself from anyone and everything social. But the burdens he faced with his ex-wife and son, Trent, made Grant emotionally tired. He didn't feel like he had much to give to another person.

Yet, watching Maurie, he realized that maybe it wasn't all about *him* giving. It was also about receiving. Everything about Maurie was unaffected. She was kind, generous, smart, and obviously talented. Not to mention beautiful. Curiosity burned through him, a feeling he hadn't had in years, and he wanted to know more about her.

Three

Maurie opened the refrigerator, trying to figure out why she'd offered Grant a drink. It would mean he'd stay longer and put his bid together in her kitchen instead of calling tomorrow or the next day with the numbers. Maurie already felt like a nervous mess around him. She'd had a major teenage crush on Grant Shelton.

He'd been a tall, gangly teenager with eyes like blue pools of water. And now he had matured into a gorgeous man. Same blue eyes, but he was taller than she remembered, and his muscular frame was a testament to his labor-intensive profession. His light-brown hair was trimmed, his face shaved, although a five o'clock shadow was making an appearance. And his nails were clean even though he worked construction. Not to mention, she'd caught his clean and spicy scent more than once as they explored the house.

She'd wondered if she was dreaming when she'd first opened the door to see Grant Shelton standing there. How many times had she thought of him after she left Pine Valley? How many men had she compared to him? More than she wanted to admit.

During her middle school and early high school years, she'd only shared a handful of words at their brief interchanges in the neighborhood. Grant had done things around their yard when he thought no one was home. He was that kind of kid, and it seemed he hadn't changed much as a man. She'd even felt the concern and generosity rolling off him as they'd walked through her house.

When Grant had done yard work at her house so many years ago, Maurie had always been home. She'd never let on that she'd seen Grant at work, because she stayed inside the house. She'd been a homeschooling recluse, and when her mom was gone Maurie had pretended no one was home. Only in the afternoons, when her mom was sleeping, had Maurie dared to sit on the porch and watch the other kids walk home from school.

So often, she'd imagined she was one of those kids walking home. She'd been in school until she was about eleven. But then her father had left, and everything had changed. Her mother had started drinking and inviting other men over. She'd slept most of the day and watched television all night. Then after an argument with the principal, she'd pulled Maurie out of school when Maurie was too young to fully understand what was going on.

Maurie remembered early mornings during the winter when Grant had shoveled snow from their walkway. He'd mowed their lawn when her mother was gone and there was been no car in the driveway. He'd probably thought Maurie was gone too. But once her mother began shoplifting and hanging out in the next town's bar, Maurie had stopped going anywhere with her.

Grant had come around the corner from his own neighborhood once when Maurie had gone out to the mailbox. He slowed down and said, "Hi, Maurie. How are you?"

Kind of formal for a teenager, but that's what made Grant Shelton different.

"Okay," she'd said. "Thanks for helping with our yard."

He'd flushed red, and Maurie stared at him, wondering what she'd said that embarrassed him.

"I—I didn't know you were home," Grant had said.

Maurie had shrugged. "I never go anywhere."

Grant had just stared at her, and she thought she saw pity in his eyes, which made her feel embarrassed. So she'd fled, running up the driveway and into the house. Like the kid she'd been.

But now she was a college graduate and ran a successful business. Of course, she could credit her foster mom and dad for showing her what normal was. Oh, and a few dozen therapy sessions in high school.

In the here and now, Maurie stared at the items in her refrigerator. Oh yeah, she was going to make a drink for Grant.

"What made you decide to return to Pine Valley?" Grant asked.

His deep tone sent a wave of warmth through her. She'd always loved his voice, the few times she'd heard it. Voices seemed to have more power over her than a man's looks. But Grant had plenty of looks as well. No doubt about that.

She turned to face him, holding a carton of cream and a pint of milk. "My mom left me the house, and well . . ." She shrugged. "After renting it out for a few years, I decided to move here and open the shop. I needed a change of scenery."

He was watching her closely. Quite intensely, in fact. It felt as if he was trying to read her thoughts.

She set the things on the counter and tucked some hair behind her ear. "Have you ever needed a do-over?"

He nodded. "Several times."

When he didn't offer more, she crossed to the kitchen table and cleared a space for him. She motioned to one of the chairs. "Have a seat. Do you need a calculator?"

He sat. "I have one on my phone."

"Oh, right." She moved back to the counter, then leaned against it and folded her arms. "What about you, Grant Shelton? What have you been up to in Pine Valley all these years?" She tried to sound lighthearted, but in truth, her heart was pounding. Here it came . . . the story about his beautiful wife and two kids. Or his live-in girlfriend who was a supermodel.

He looked up from the list. "Uh, that's a depressing tale."

Depressing? Not what she expected at all. Grant Shelton didn't seem like he had a depressing life. Everything about him seemed on the ball. From his looks to his clothing to his professionalism.

"Hmm," she said. "I think a depressing tale deserves something sweet." She took the dark-chocolate mix out of the cupboard and poured milk into a pan. She felt his gaze on her, and Maurie tried to keep the smile off her face. She'd intrigued him. Good.

"You're making me *hot chocolate*?" he asked.

She glanced over at his expression and laughed. "Cocoa," she clarified. "And you've never tasted anything like it, believe me. Besides, I want to hear your depressing tale."

He visibly swallowed, and a thought hit her. Maybe he was as nervous as she felt.

"All right," he said, looking down at the paper in front of him, then back up at her. One of his brows cocked, and she didn't know what to make of that expression. "If you're sure you want to hear it."

She held his gaze. The old Maurie would have shied away from such a personal conversation. But she was no longer that girl. "I'd love to."

His gaze moved over her face, then he propped his elbows on the table and released a sigh. "It's not for the faint of heart."

The way he said it made her want to smile. But she refrained for now. She turned on the burner until the gas flame leapt to life. After mixing in the cream and several scoops of dark-chocolate powder, she lowered the temperature to a simmer and turned to face him. "I'm listening."

Grant scrubbed a hand through his hair, leaving it mussed. "So, right now I'm in a custody battle for my four-year-old son. His mother wants to keep him in another city and raise him with another man."

Maurie stared at him for a second before she realized staring was probably rude. "Oh. Wow. Sorry." She moved to the table, shoved a few things aside, and sat across from Grant. He was divorced, and he was a father. "What's your son's name?"

He looked surprised at her question. "Trent."

"Trent Shelton," she said. "Great name. He'll be a strong and good man, like his father."

Grant held her gaze for a moment. "That's a pretty big prediction. You haven't even met the kid."

Maurie didn't have to meet the kid. She didn't even have to meet Grant's ex-wife. "A kid takes after the good parent," she said in a quiet voice. "Believe me, I know. My father might have left us, but I think I must be like him. I am nothing like my mother."

The atmosphere in the kitchen had shifted into something else—like an understanding between close friends.

"You are nothing like your mother," Grant said, his tone also subdued. "Are you . . . are you doing okay after all that happened?"

Not many people knew about her life in Pine Valley, or

at least what it had really been like. Maurie couldn't guess what exactly Grant knew, but he probably had a decent understanding. "I'm doing okay. I've been able to move past a lot of things. And I know that fixing up this house is going to make a difference too."

Grant nodded. "Well, you've impressed me."

"I have?" Maurie felt the heat rising in her neck. "I don't know what you're basing that on."

Grant smiled. It was sort of a sad smile though. "Just an instinct. And I appreciate your compliment about my son. It's been hard to see past the court battles to a time when I can just be a regular dad to him without all the tension between me and my ex. I had Trent for three days over Christmas, and now I won't see him until spring break."

Maurie could very well guess that his son was a sweet, adorable boy. And she saw in Grant's gaze how much he loved his kid. "When's spring break?"

"Middle of March."

The sound of the hot cocoa coming to a boil alerted Maurie. She stood and crossed to the stove, then stirred the cocoa. "Three months is a long time for a little kid. Can you call him at night?"

"Joy usually tells me he's asleep," Grant said. "Going through her can be impossible."

Maurie wanted to curse out his ex-wife. Who does that? Maurie turned down the flame beneath the pan. "Does Trent have an iPad or a phone?"

"He has an iPad," Grant said, his tone curious.

Maurie looked over at him with a smile. "Perfect. Then you can FaceTime."

Grant's brows rose. "Is that like Facebook?"

"No . . ." She laughed. "I take it you're not on social media."

Grant shook his head. "Uh, no. I hate social media."

She smirked. "Me too. But it's a great way to reach my customers. So I bow to the almighty dollar, I guess." She removed the pan from the burner, then crossed to the table. "Here, let me see your phone."

He handed it over, and she turned on FaceTime in his settings, then handed it back.

She pulled out her own phone from her back pocket, then asked, "What's your number?" She typed in the number he recited, then she FaceTimed him.

Grant stared at his ringing phone. "What do I do?" he asked.

She crossed to him and leaned over his shoulder, then pointed at the Answer button. "Swipe, then hold the phone in front of your face."

He did, and his eyes widened.

"Hi, Grant," she said into her phone, smiling at his image on the screen.

"Hi." He stood and walked about the small kitchen, angling his phone this way and that, experimenting with her image.

"Is the bid ready yet?" Maurie asked as Grant brought his phone really close to his face until only one blue eye filled her screen.

He laughed at his copied image in the corner of his phone, the sound sending warm prickles along her skin. "I haven't started yet," he said. "You've been too distracting."

They held each other's gazes in their phones for a few seconds.

"Sorry?" Maurie said at last, lowering her phone.

"It's okay," Grant said, his gaze sliding to her actual face. "It's a nice distraction."

Maurie was proud of herself for not blushing, but that

didn't stop the butterflies in her stomach. "I'll leave you to your estimate and finish getting this cocoa ready."

He returned to the table and sat down, but Maurie didn't miss the half smile on his face as he opened the calculator on his phone.

Well then. She went back to stirring the cooling chocolate mixture that was still steaming. She pulled down two mugs from the cupboard. The mugs were different patterns and shapes, since she never bought two exactly alike.

Maurie worked in silence, only hearing the scratch of Grant's pencil against the notepaper. She poured the cocoa into the mugs, careful not to fill them too much, to leave plenty of room for the sweeter stuff.

She heard Grant exhale, and she looked over her shoulder. "Everything okay?"

He glanced up, then looked down again at the notepaper. "It's going to take at least two weeks, maybe longer."

"That's not a problem," she said. "When can you get started?"

"Does tomorrow work?"

"Perfect." She poured the steaming cocoa and then used a peppermint stick in each to stir. Leaving the peppermint sticks in the mugs, she topped each with a dollop of whipped cream and a sprinkle of cinnamon.

She picked up one of the mugs and turned to present it to Grant, only to find that he'd crossed the room and was standing near her.

"Can I help you?" he said, then his gaze landed on the mug. "Wow, this is too fancy to drink."

Maurie looked into his blue eyes. "I can make you another if you'd just like to look at that one," she teased.

"No." His gaze held hers before he grinned. "I'm drinking this."

So, standing right there in front of her, he took a sip and

swallowed. "It's like perfection." He leaned against the counter, his shoulder only inches from hers.

Was it just her, or had this kitchen shrunk in size? She could smell his clean, spicy scent, and mixed with the aroma of chocolate and peppermint, it was like walking into a holiday festival.

"How did you do this?" Grant continued.

Maurie shrugged as if to act as if it was no big deal. But truthfully, she was flattered at Grant's interest. "Years of practice. My foster mother was a gourmet cook. You should have seen her meals—even the simple ones. I was pretty desperate for a normal mom, so I stayed with her in the kitchen after school and on the weekends, instead of being social."

Grant took another sip of his drink. "Your foster mom sounds pretty great."

Maurie's throat tightened. "She was. She passed away a few years ago."

Grant set his mug on the counter. "I'm sorry. I didn't know."

How could he know?

"And your mom too," he said. "I heard about her passing."

Maurie drank from her own cocoa before answering. The hot sweetness was instantly soothing. "Yeah. I still haven't been to her gravesite. Maybe someday."

Grant didn't say anything for a minute, and Maurie wondered if she'd gotten too personal, too fast. But he had known her mom, so maybe it was okay.

"Maurie," he said, his voice low. "I'm sorry about all of your losses." He rested a hand on her shoulder.

She wanted to lean into him, because the comfort of his hand on her shoulder made her eyes burn with tears. Not even her foster parents had known her mother. So to have this connection with another person who did know her, and was certainly aware of all her faults, was new to Maurie.

She placed her hand over his. "Thanks." Their gazes locked, and Maurie could swear he was leaning closer, but then his phone rang from its place on the table.

Grant moved to pick up his phone. He sent the caller into voicemail, then he turned to face her. "Thanks for showing me the FaceTime thing. Trent's going to love it."

Maurie nodded, still feeling a lump in her throat. "I hope so."

He picked up the bid sheet and handed it to her. "See what you think of the estimate."

She took the sheet and scanned the numbers. All of the prices looked fair. "Looks good."

Grant moved past her and walked to the sink, where he rinsed out his mug.

"You don't have to wash . . ." she started, but he was finished before she could protest.

"No problem." He set the mug on the counter. "Thanks again, and I'll be here around eight a.m. tomorrow if that's not too early."

"Sounds great."

Grant nodded and took the bid sheet. He seemed to be hesitating. Waiting for something.

"Look, Maurie," he said, his blue gaze holding hers. "If you need help with anything . . . else, besides your house, let me know."

Maurie could only nod. She couldn't fathom what had possessed Grant's ex-wife to give him up. He was about the most decent guy she knew.

"See you early tomorrow," he continued. Then he left the kitchen and walked out the front door before Maurie could find her voice.

Four

As Grant strode to his truck, he knew he was in big trouble. First of all, Maurie didn't know he was the one who'd changed her life. Because of him, she'd been put into foster care. Fortunately, it seemed she'd had amazing foster parents, and that might be why she seemed so successful now. Although, there was still baggage over her real mother. Maurie hadn't even visited the woman's grave.

Second, being around Maurie for less than an hour had brought up thoughts that had long been buried by Joy. Thoughts of what it might be like to date Maurie, to really get to know her. To become a part of her life. She was beautiful, there was no doubt, and he was definitely attracted to her.

Therein lay the problem. Grant would be spending hours at Maurie's house over the next few weeks, and they'd likely have many encounters. It wouldn't be fair not to tell her about his role in her last night in Pine Valley.

Grant climbed into his truck. The wintry air had turned sharp, and he cranked on the heater. He took a final look at the house before pulling away from the curb. Had he done the right thing ten years ago? Looking at how successful and seemingly content Maurie was now, he could probably talk himself into believing it had all been for the best. But a short visit with her couldn't erase ten years of questions and guilt. There had to be much more that she wasn't telling him. If the roles had been reversed, he couldn't imagine what he might be feeling.

Grant turned the corner, heading to his last appointment of the day as a dusting of snow fell from the dark-gray sky. He'd spent the last two weeks building and painting cupboards for Mrs. Jones, two blocks over. Today he'd mount all of the cupboards and install the hardware. He couldn't wait to see the finished product, and it would be a welcome distraction to take his thoughts away from the beautiful woman he'd just spent time with.

When Grant stopped in front of Mrs. Jones's house, he let the truck idle for a couple of minutes as he gathered his thoughts. Should he tell Maurie that he'd been the one to call the cops on her mom? Wouldn't it only bring more pain and dredge up bad memories? Mind made up, he shut off the engine and climbed out.

Mrs. Jones greeted him at the door, a smile on her cheerful, round face and a plate of muffins in hand.

"Bless you, Mrs. Jones," he said with a grin. "I'm starving."

"You're too thin for a full-grown man," Mrs. Jones said. "I baked these special for you. From one of those mixes, but I didn't think you'd mind."

"I don't mind." Grant walked with her into the kitchen and ate two muffins before he started the install. As he worked, he could hear the hum of a game show on television.

It reminded him of time spent at his own grandparents' house when he was a kid. The warmth of the house, the smell of homemade goods, and the drone of the television on a cold winter afternoon. Grant thought of Maurie and how she didn't even have grandparents.

The install went smoothly, and Mrs. Jones insisted on writing him a check then and there.

"Thank you, Mrs. Jones," he said. "Be sure to call us if there's anything else you need."

Mrs. Jones patted his arm. "You are a dear. Thank you, my boy. And be sure to take the rest of the muffins. I'm more of a donut gal."

Grant laughed and took the paper plate she offered.

He left the warmth and kindness of Mrs. Jones's house, only to arrive home to the dark and cold apartment he called his own.

As he flipped on the kitchen light, a reminder popped up on his cell phone. He'd forgotten about dinner with his sister, Julie. He was no longer starving, thanks to the muffins; besides, he had some research to do. So he texted Julie that he wouldn't make dinner. He turned up the thermostat a notch and settled at his kitchen table, where he turned on his too-slow laptop and googled Maurie Ledbetter.

Before he knew it, he'd spent two hours clicking on links associated with her name. She'd graduated high school with honors and earned a Bachelor of Arts degree in college. When he poked around on her Facebook page, he unearthed only a few pictures. To see more he'd need to friend her. But she looked happy and healthy and successful from what he saw.

Grant shut off the laptop and leaned back in his chair. Night had deepened around him, and his apartment felt emptier than normal. At least Maurie would have a roommate soon. Yet he thought about all of her losses—and they were all significant.

The guilt that churned in his stomach would fade with

time. Right? He'd spend the next couple of weeks fixing up her house while she'd put together her shop. How much would he really see her anyway? After his job was completed he might see her once in a while about the town, but to have a congenial relationship with her, it wasn't as if he needed to bare his soul.

Besides, he had his own issues to deal with. Telling Maurie about his part in her past might only give her an additional burden. So he'd re-focus on his own problems.

He reached for his phone and pulled up Joy's number. Calling his ex-wife was his least favorite thing to do, but for now it was the only way to get through to Trent. Grant hoped FaceTime would change all of that.

"Grant, it's late," Joy said with no preamble.

He glanced at the microwave digital clock. It was 8:45 p.m., later than he'd thought. "Is Trent still awake?"

Joy sighed. "You know I don't want his bedtime routine messed up. He's reading books with Stone."

Something in Grant's heart pinched. As much as he couldn't stand Stone, Grant wanted to be the one putting Trent to bed each night. "I'll keep it short," Grant said. He waited for her to argue, and he wouldn't be surprised if she did. But the fact that Joy had answered the phone in the first place told him she was in a generous mood.

"All right," she said, not bothering to hide the exasperation in her tone. "Ten minutes tops."

Grant didn't have a chance to reply, and while he was waiting for Joy to take the phone to Trent, Grant wondered how his life had gone from being married and taking care of Trent most of the time to being told that he could only be a dad for ten minutes at a time. If there had been any way to save his marriage, Grant would have done it. Hell, he'd been the one to suggest counseling, and he was always bending backwards to meet every single one of Joy's demands. But in the end, Grant's profession and simple lifestyle weren't enough for Joy.

"Daddy?" Trent's small voice came through the phone.

All of Grant's dark thoughts disintegrated in a second. "Hey, buddy. Are you getting ready for bed?"

"Yeah, I'm reading a joke book."

Grant chuckled even though his heart ached. "Sounds cool. Can you tell me a joke?"

"Okay." Trent paused. "What has ears but can't hear?"

"Um . . ." Grant stalled. "I have no idea."

Trent giggled. "A cornfield. Get it?"

Grant laughed. "I get it."

"Want to hear another one?"

"Yeah, in a second," Grant said. "I want to try something first. Can you get your iPad?"

When Trent got his iPad, Grant told him how to turn on FaceTime in the settings. "I'm going to hang up and call you, okay? Do you know how to answer?"

Seconds later, Grant was gazing at Trent's face on his phone.

"I can see you, Daddy!" Trent said.

"And I can see you," Grant said with a grin. "How about I call you every night at eight thirty on your iPad, and you can tell me any new jokes."

"Okey-dokey," Trent said. "Ready for the next one?"

Grant would always be ready.

They spent the next ten minutes talking and laughing as Trent told Grant his jokes.

By the time Grant hung up with Trent, he felt less empty. Less alone. This FaceTime thing was going to make a big difference, and he had Maurie to thank for it.

Five

When Grant awakened the next morning, he knew something was different. At first he wasn't sure what it was, and then he remembered all the events from the day before. Namely, Maurie Ledbetter. He hoped she'd be home when he arrived at her house, because he wanted to thank her for the FaceTime idea.

With his labor-intensive work, Grant didn't bother with going to the gym or running the streets unless it was the weekend. So he showered and was ready quickly. He grabbed a coffee from the gas station on his way to Maurie's and arrived a few minutes after eight.

As Grant climbed out of his truck, the old doubts returned. Maybe he should tell her about calling the cops on her mother. No . . . he'd been over this in his mind already. It might only bring her more stress and doubts and second-guessing. Maurie was in a good place, and he didn't want to mess that up.

Grant lugged the toolbox out of the bed of his truck and strode up the walkway. Once he reached the front door, he knocked. When no one answered, he knocked again. There was at least one light on inside, so that gave him hope. Still, what if she'd left to do something? He looked for a note, but there was nothing. So he tried the doorknob and found it unlocked.

"Maurie?" he called as he stepped inside.

The scent of something baking wafted past him. Bread, maybe? His stomach tightened, letting him know that coffee was never enough. But the house was quiet. Had Maurie left the oven on?

"It's Grant. I'm here to start working." Still nothing.

He glanced toward the kitchen, surprised to see the mug of hot chocolate that she'd drunk from still on the table.

"Maurie?" He moved into the hallway, and then he heard her voice.

"Grant?"

The sound came from above . . . the attic? He strode toward the sound and saw the open hatch in the corner of the second bedroom.

Two feet dangled from the opening.

As he moved toward the hatch, Maurie's legs appeared, clad in black leggings. "Can you help me down? I'm getting vertigo."

"Okay," Grant said, looking up. "Move as close to the edge as possible, and I'll hold your legs while you lower yourself to the chair."

She scooted to the edge of the hatch, and dust filtered down. Grant blinked against the dust and grasped Maurie's legs. He tried not to think about their close proximity.

"I feel sick," Maurie said.

"Like *sick* sick, or you just hate heights?" Grant asked.

"I don't know."

"Come on, I've got you." He wrapped his arms more fully about her legs to give her more support. "Let go."

She did.

Good thing Grant had braced his legs so that he didn't topple against the wall, because he hadn't expected her to pretty much let herself drop. She didn't even come close to landing on the chair.

Maurie yelped, and Grant staggered but remained upright. He set her down, keeping his arms about her to steady her. "Are you okay?"

Maurie's green eyes were wide; her dark waves had been pulled into a knot, but tendrils of curls created a wild halo about her head. Streaks of dust crossed her cheeks, and dirt stained her oversized shirt.

"Thank you," Maurie said, her hands on his shoulders.

Her body was warm and curvy and soft in the places a woman was soft. Grant swallowed. And released her.

"What were you doing up there?" he asked.

Maurie brushed at her clothing. "I, uh—" She sneezed.

"Bless you," he said, holding back a smile. He plucked out a wad of lint from her hair.

"You came just in time to rescue me." She brushed something off his shoulder, and his heart tripped again. "Sorry about the dust. I was checking to see if my mom had put anything up there."

He stepped back because they were standing very, very close. Even though she was grimy from the attic, she was even more beautiful than she had been yesterday.

"Find anything?" he asked.

She smiled. "I did. I've been up there for over an hour looking through old albums that my grandmother probably put together. Pictures I've never seen."

"Really?" He rested his hands on his hips, trying to gauge her reaction to seeing old pictures of her family. She didn't look upset or anything. "Do you want me to bring them down?"

"Thanks. But you don't have to go up there."

He lifted his hands. "Free of charge."

She studied him as if she was doubting.

"It will take only a couple of minutes," he said.

The edges of her mouth curved. "All right, I'd appreciate that."

"No problem." He stepped onto the chair and poked his head through the hatch opening. It took a few seconds for his eyes to adjust to the dimness. More boxes stacked. Odds and ends of furniture. The attic's mustiness attacked, and he sneezed.

"It's really dirty," Maurie called up, amusement in her tone.

"I got it." Grant braced his elbows on the edges and pulled himself up with a grunt. He slowly straightened in the cramped space, then he spotted some opened boxes. Sure enough, they contained photo albums. There were about a dozen other boxes—handmade boxes, with their taped edges and corners. A small crib that was more of a bassinet stood in one corner. And a huge stack of *National Geographic* magazines teetered in another corner. Grant picked up the top magazine. 1968.

He flipped through a few pages, then he picked up the box with photo albums. He crossed to the hatch opening.

Maurie was standing on the chair, waiting.

"I'll hand down the box to you." He knelt and lowered the box into her waiting arms. "Do you want both boxes?"

"Yep."

"Did you see all of these *National Geographic*s up here?"

"Yeah, I think they were my grandpa's," she said, gazing up at him. "He died when I was pretty young, so I don't remember much."

He rested his hands on his knees. "Well, if you want someone to take them off your hands, let me know."

"You want them?" Her brows lifted.

He shrugged. "Only if you don't."

She smiled, and it did something funny to his heart. "They're all yours, Grant Shelton. Hand them down too."

So he did, right after he grabbed the other box of photo albums. By the time Grant had lowered himself down through the hatch, he was even dirtier than Maurie.

"Look at you," she said, brushing at his sleeve. "Do you need to go home and get cleaned up?"

He looked down at his dusty clothing. "I'm used to these working conditions. Unless you'd rather I clean up?"

"Oh, no, you're fine," Maurie said. "The dust is making me itchy though, so I'm getting in the shower. Help yourself to the cinnamon rolls."

"Did you say cinnamon rolls?" Grant asked.

Maurie laughed. "Sure did. Made them this morning."

Grant stared at her. "Homemade?"

She brushed off her hands. "Sure thing. Got up at five to mix the dough."

"Five in the morning?"

She set her hands on her hips. "Yeah. It's about a two-and-a-half-hour process."

Grant rubbed the back of his neck. "Wow. Would it be too forward if I asked you to marry me?"

Maurie grinned. "What? Your wife didn't cook?" She slapped a hand over her mouth. "Sorry, that was really rude."

Grant wasn't offended in the least. "Joy was really great at ordering takeout. Which was fine. I mean, theoretically *I* could have cooked."

Maurie's brows lifted. "*Do* you cook?"

"I can warm up chili from a can." He winked. "And make a mean PB&J."

She patted him on the chest and moved past him into the

hallway. "Well, enjoy the cinnamon rolls. There's milk in the fridge too."

Grant made a beeline for the kitchen. He rounded the corner and stepped into paradise. Well, the kitchen was still a disaster, but the cleared portion of the kitchen counter was topped with a baking pan with lightly browned cinnamon rolls. It took him about ten seconds to find a spatula in a fancy floral vase, and another ten seconds to bite into the soft goodness.

He ate an entire cinnamon roll before locating a glass and pouring himself milk. Then he ate a second roll. He could have easily eaten a third, but he wondered if Maurie had plans for the others. When his mother baked, she took half to a neighbor's. Said it helped keep her waist trim.

He'd decided to start working in the kitchen, so that part could be functional first. Besides, by the sound of it, Maurie was in the only bathroom in the house, so he couldn't very well work there. He went outside to grab the saw table from the back of his truck. He set it up on the porch and cut new shelves for the pantry. The ones she had were unsalvageable.

When he brought them into the kitchen, the shower was running, and he tried not to think of Maurie in the shower, only a couple of walls away. Too distracting. He needed music on or something. Maybe he'd download a couple of audio books to listen to.

The shower shut off, and Grant shook his head, chasing his imagination away. Just because she was an attractive woman didn't mean that there would be a relationship between them. He couldn't imagine dating someone he kept such a huge secret from. And if he told her, he didn't think she'd be as friendly.

But he liked being around Maurie, as little time as it had been. He hadn't allowed himself to relax around a woman in a long time. Since his divorce, Grant had gone on exactly two dates—one was set up and the other a spur-of-the-moment connection. Neither had led to second dates. But now it was all that he could do to not let his imagination get away from him as he thought about what it would be like to take Maurie out for dinner, or on a long walk near the ski resort, or for a coffee at the Main Street Café.

"Snap out of it," he mumbled as he hammered the two-by-four that would hold the new pantry shelf.

"Did you say something?" Maurie asked.

He turned to see her standing in the kitchen doorway. Her skin gleamed pink from her shower, making her eyes bright. Her hair was still wet, with small water droplets marking the shoulders of her long-sleeved shirt. She wore ratty jeans with holes at the knees, the jeans fitting her curves as if they'd been painted on.

Well. "Uh, I should have warned you," he said, swallowing hard. "I talk to myself when I work."

"Hmm," Maurie said with a smirk. "I'll be sure to stay close by then." She crossed the kitchen, and his gaze followed her.

She cut a cinnamon roll from the pan.

"Those were delicious, by the way," he said. "Thank you."

She took a bite without answering, then looked over at him. "You're welcome. There's plenty here if you want more." Her gaze flitted down his body.

The back of his neck heated. And . . . he realized he was staring as she took another bite. He could practically taste the cinnamon and sugar himself. He forced his gaze to the pantry. *Back to work.*

"By the way, I FaceTimed Trent last night, and he loved it." Grant positioned the last shelf to mark where he'd hammer in the brackets. It was a bit tricky to make the markings with one hand balancing the shelf.

"Good to hear," Maurie said, close to his ear. "Here, I'll hold the shelf."

He hadn't realized she'd crossed the room. But now she was right beside him, her peppermint scent dominating his senses.

She reached up and balanced the shelf, and he could practically feel her warmth against his skin even though they weren't touching.

He marked the location for the brackets, wishing it took more than a few seconds to do so. "Thanks," he said, grasping the shelf.

She smiled and let it go. He set the shelf on the floor.

"So your son liked FaceTime, huh?"

There was a small bit of cinnamon at the edge of her mouth, and Grant couldn't take his eyes from it. "Yes. He loved it, and I loved seeing his face while we talked. Well, I sort of hated it too, because it made me miss him more. But now I don't have to go through Joy every time I want to get in touch with my kid."

"Nice," Maurie said, and she moved past him, out of the pantry area.

Their arms brushed, and the hairs on his arms stood up.

"I'm glad it worked out," Maurie said.

"Me too," Grant said.

"I should get through my emails," Maurie said. "Let me know if you need anything. I'll be in my bedroom."

"Will do." Grant watched her walk out of the kitchen, the feel of her arm against his still lingering. Then he went back to work before he allowed himself to get even more distracted.

Six

While Grant hammered away in the kitchen, Maurie texted Taffy. *Just a warning. An old friend of mine is doing repair work on the house. Grant Shelton. And I'm only going to tell you once. I'm not interested in him.*

Her phone rang thirty seconds later.

"*Grant Shelton?*" Taffy practically shouted. "The neighbor guy who used to mow your lawn when your mom was gone?"

Maurie groaned. She'd told Taffy about her past in Pine Valley, and apparently that had included all about Grant too.

"Is he still drop-dead gorgeous?" Taffy pressed.

Maurie climbed off her bed to shut her bedroom door. "Is that how I described him?"

"Pretty much." Taffy laughed. "So what's his story? Is he married?"

"Divorced, with a kid. In the middle of a custody battle." Maurie crossed the room and looked through the small window at the overgrown backyard. Even in the winter, the place was a jungle. "And yes, he's still gorgeous, but before you say anything, he's like a million miles away emotionally, and *no*... I'm not interested. When I start dating again, it's going to be someone with no baggage. I have enough of my own for two."

Taffy scoffed. "Yeah, good luck with that, Maurie. You're twenty-seven. What are you going to do, marry a twenty-year-old? Every guy your age will have baggage. And if they haven't been married or in a serious relationship, then you probably don't want anything to do with them."

Maurie sighed. This was not the first lecture she had received from Taffy on this topic. "Okay, okay, when you put it like that—"

"When I put it like what?" Taffy lowered her voice. "Are you admitting that you're still *attracted* to Mr. Hot Guy?"

"Don't call him that." Maurie turned away from the window as a drill sounded from the kitchen. She wondered what Grant was drilling. "I mean, Grant is a *dad*."

"Oh my heck, girl, you've still got it for him," Taffy said, delight in her voice. "I can't *wait* to meet him. Which will be, incidentally, in about seven hours."

Maurie sat on her bed and leaned against the pillows. "He won't be here in seven hours," she said.

"Then tomorrow," Taffy said, amusement in her tone.

Maurie exhaled. "Well, I can't wait to see you. I think this whole shop-owner thing will feel *real* once you're here and we can start moving everything into the shop."

"I know, I can't wait," Taffy said. "See you soon."

Once Maurie hung up, she listened for a few minutes to the sound of whatever high-pitched drill Grant was using. What *was* he doing? Curiosity got the better of her. Climbing off her bed, she checked her reflection in the mirror above the dresser. Her hair had dried in a riot of curls, so she smoothed it back and knotted it into a ponytail.

She found Grant in the living room, removing screws from the dark wood paneling that lined the walls. Several panel pieces already lay on the floor. Grant had taken off the flannel shirt he'd worn over a navy T-shirt. His forearms were strangely tanned for the middle of winter and not-so-strangely muscled.

"You're taking the paneling off?" she asked when there was a short break in the noise. "I thought you were going to paint over it."

He glanced at her, then he bent to pick up one of the panel pieces. When he turned it over, she saw the black on the other side.

"I think it's mold," he said. "But it looks like it's only embedded on the paneling and not the walls."

"Oh, wow." She walked closer. "I'm glad you caught that."

"With material this old, I have to check." Grant scanned the rest of the room, and then his blue gaze settled on hers. "If you need help taking your boxes to the shop, I've got a truck."

Maurie noticed a light sheen of perspiration on his forehead and his arms and . . . "Well, that would be nice, but my friend Taffy is arriving tonight. We'll probably rent a trailer."

Grant lifted a single brow. "You don't need to rent a trailer. My truck can handle it."

Maurie tilted her head. "Don't you think the work will go faster if you do the house stuff and I do the store stuff?"

The edges of Grant's mouth twitched as if he was holding back a smile. "Since I have to remove the paneling sooner than later, I was thinking we could take a truckload over today. It's a bit crowded in here."

Maurie followed his gaze. Boxes were everywhere. She couldn't really expect him to work when there was hardly room to walk. She looked back to him to find that he was watching her. "I don't want to put you out," she said. "And I'm not sure if I can really move stuff into the shop until I officially close."

"Why don't you call the realtor?" Grant said. "Is it Jeff Finch?"

How many realtors were there? "Yeah, do you know him?"

Grant smiled. "It's Pine Valley. We go back a ways. Let me know what he says."

"Okay," Maurie said, not entirely convinced she wanted to be that pushy.

Grant turned to the next part of the panel and started up his drill again.

Well then. Grant was a bit bossy, it seemed. But she'd hired him to do the renovations, so she returned to her bedroom, shut the door, and called the realtor.

Jeff Finch answered on the second ring. "Finch Realty," he answered.

"Hi, uh, Jeff," she said. "It's Maurie Ledbetter. I'm wondering if it would be okay if I moved some boxes into the store space today. I've got Grant Shelton at my house doing renovations, and we could use the extra room."

Jeff didn't hesitate. "Sure thing. Stop by my office on your way, and I'll have the key ready for you. You can keep the key, but you'll need to let me know each time you're going to use it."

"No problem," she told the realtor. "Thanks for this. Grant will be happy too."

"I get it. How's he doing, by the way?"

"Fine, I think." The turn in the conversation surprised her. Things with Jeff Finch had never veered toward personal before. Even though she knew there was no way Grant could overhear the conversation, she lowered her voice. "Should I be worried about him?"

"Oh, it's nothing, I'm sure," Jeff said. "He's cancelled on everything that we've tried to set up with the guys. We go way back to high school. Since his divorce, I've reached out to him a few times, but no dice."

Maurie swallowed. "I don't know Grant well enough to comment. Although he did mention some frustrations with the custody issues over his son."

"Yeah, Trent's a great kid," Jeff said. "Sorry. Don't mean to get you involved."

"It's okay," she said. "I'm here to stay in Pine Valley, and if there are things I can help with, I'm happy to."

"We're excited to have you, Maurie," Jeff said, his tone warm. "See you soon."

After she hung up with Jeff, she thought about what he'd said about Grant. If he had isolated himself from pretty much everyone, he probably wasn't dating. It was interesting to think about, and it sort of made her feel fluttery. And guilty at the same time. Fluttery that he was available and guilty because he seemed to be under a lot of stress.

So, it looked like she'd be moving boxes right now with Grant.

She walked into the living room. Grant had worked fast and had removed the paneling along an entire wall. He glanced over and, seeing her, turned off his drill.

"The realtor gave us the green light," she said. "We just need to pick up the key from his office."

"Great." Grant unplugged the drill and set it on the floor. "Which boxes do you want to go first?"

She looked around the room. "Everything in this room goes, except for the baskets. I'll be doing some orders over the weekend."

"Great," he said, then picked up a double set of boxes.

Maurie opened the door for him. "I'll grab my shoes and jacket, then help." She hurried to her bedroom and pulled on her tennis shoes, then found a zip-up jacket in her closet. She didn't want to wear a full coat or she'd get too hot.

Twenty minutes later, the bed of Grant's truck was loaded with boxes. And while she was trying to catch her breath, he closed the tailgate and then jumped into the truck.

She climbed in, noticing that he didn't look the least bit winded. He wasn't even perspiring, and he was still in his T-shirt. Which meant Maurie couldn't let herself stare at him too long. Apparently her teen crush hadn't completely died. She was just glad he wasn't married anymore; it would have been even more awkward crushing on him.

"How did you get into gift-basket sales?" he asked, pulling away from the curb.

Maurie leaned back on the seat. His truck was older, but it was clean and had a polish scent to it as if he cleaned it regularly. "Probably something to do with my foster mom. Not only was she a fabulous chef, but she always put together the most amazing presentations for neighbor gifts and fundraisers."

Grant nodded. "So you started out as a dot.com?"

"Yeah, I loved the flexibility of filling orders," she said. "Day or night. But I soon learned that it was hard to shut off work . . . you know, I'd never really get a break because my job was at home."

"I can imagine," Grant said. "Most people don't like hammering in their house late into the night, so my job definitely has a cutoff time. Do you have only one employee?"

"For now," Maurie said. "I'd like to hire someone part-time in Pine Valley. Taffy will continue to do most of the online stuff. So I'll focus on the retail location. Unless I can convince Taffy to move here. She always talks about the day she wants to settle down and have a bunch of kids, so a small town is perfect for that."

"What about you? Did you come to Pine Valley to settle down and have kids?" Grant asked, then his neck stained red. "I mean," he backtracked, "that didn't come out right."

Maurie looked out the window, willing her own blush to stay away. "It's okay," she said. "I suppose if it happens, then it happens. But if there's one thing I learned in my months of therapy, it's to be happy wherever I am. Happiness comes from my choices in life and not from worrying about what is beyond my control." She exhaled. Had she said too much? Been too personal?

She peeked at him to see that he was smiling.

When their gazes connected, he said, "You're pretty amazing, you know that?"

Heat stole across her cheeks. Well, she was definitely blushing now. "You're pretty great too. As a kid, and now." Before she could dig herself any deeper, she added, "You have way more energy than I'll ever have."

Grant smiled as he turned the final corner that led to Main Street. "Working hard keeps my mind off the other stuff."

Boy, did Maurie know that. She didn't want to keep quoting her therapist, so she said, "I completely get that."

Grant slowed the truck in front of the realtor's office. The lights were on, and through the window Maurie spotted a pretty, red-haired woman. She must be the receptionist.

"I'll grab the key." Maurie opened the door and climbed out of the truck just as Mr. Finch came out the front door.

"Hello there, Maurie." He held up the key as he walked toward the truck. He peered around her. "Grant. How's it going?"

Maurie took the key and stood aside as Jeff moved to the open door to talk to Grant.

"Keeping busy, Jeff," Grant said. "How about you?"

"Work, as usual," Jeff said. "Hey, are you up for skiing next weekend?"

"About that . . ." Grant said in a hesitant voice. "I've got a lot of work going on, so I'd better not commit to anything."

Jeff patted the doorframe of the truck. "No problem. If you change your mind, even at the last minute, shoot me a text or give me a call."

The two men said goodbye, and soon Grant and Maurie were on their way again.

"So you ski?" she asked.

"Yeah," he said, but he didn't elaborate.

"If you think I expect you to work weekends at my house, I don't," Maurie said. "It will probably be good for you to do something other than work."

"Like I said, I'd rather work than much else at this point." He paused. "Sorry, I'm not . . . Well, I was married, and I really don't feel like I fit into the single life anymore. Skiing all day, then going to the bar and picking up women isn't really on my priority list."

"Maybe you can skip the bar part," Maurie said. She didn't know why she was pushing so much. Grant's activities were none of her business.

"Maybe." Grant's tone was noncommittal.

Maurie thought about Jeff Finch. He was a good-looking man, though not someone she was really attracted to, and she hadn't considered what his personal life might be like. But what else did handsome, single men do on the weekends?

Grant drummed his fingers on the steering wheel, then pulled over to the corner where her shop was located.

Before shutting off the engine, he looked over at her. "I'm

way past high school, if you know what I mean. The pickup scene at bars gets really old, really fast. Reminds me of high school stag dances."

Maurie nodded. "I never really got the regular high school experience."

"Yeah, and I'm sorry for that," he said. "I wish things could have been different for you, even though I'd be the first to say you didn't miss much."

Maurie's throat tightened.

"But there is something to say for going through all the rites of adolescent passage," Grant said in a soft voice.

She pushed back the emotion that was welling up inside of her. "Well, like you said, I missed out on all those horror stories from high school," she said. "Gladys thought I should continue with homeschooling because I didn't have time to catch up and attend regular classes. So college was my first classroom experience since middle school." Her voice sounded overly bright, and she knew it.

"If you could do things all over again, what would you wish for?" Grant's tone was somber, and he still hadn't turned off the ignition.

She looked away from his blue gaze, then down at her clasped hands. "A mom who cared about me from the beginning until the end." Now the tears weren't going to stay away. She blinked a few times. "In the end, I did get that. Even if for only a few years, and even if she wasn't my biological mom. I was lucky for the time I had with her." She brushed at her cheeks. "Sorry, I guess this moving stuff has made me emotional."

Grant rested a hand on her shoulder, and the warm weight of his palm was comforting. It also sped up her heart rate. His fingers brushed against her neck, and Maurie inhaled at the sensation.

"I don't blame you," Grant said. "You're doing a brave thing. Changes are always hard, yet here you are, moving mountains."

She let a small smile escape. She wanted to lean into his touch. Feel more of his warmth. Instead, she reached for the door and popped it open. "Back to work, Grant Shelton."

She loved the way his eyes crinkled at the corners when he smiled.

Grant turned off the engine, then opened his own door.

They climbed out, and Maurie crossed the sidewalk to the front door of her shop. She'd have to scrape off the stenciling on the door and change it to *Every Occasion*. Maybe Taffy would do it.

Maurie unlocked the door to the shop, then held the door open as Grant carried in the first stack of boxes. He carried boxes two at a time, while she only managed one. With Grant's help, the work went fast. Once all the boxes had been unloaded, Maurie closed the propped door and surveyed the bare walls.

Grant came to stand next to her. "This is the place, huh?"

"Yep." Maurie felt the slow warmth of joy seep through her. This *was* the place. *Her* place.

The shop had been cleaned out by the previous owners. But there was some trash on the ground, and the main counter was in a sorry state. It had been a clothing boutique. Framed posters of models had been taken down, leaving a dingy outline on the taupe walls. Maurie had already decided to paint the walls a soft yellow to give a warm and friendly ambience.

"What are your plans?" he asked.

And she knew he wasn't asking out of politeness. As she told him of her design ideas, he nodded along the way, asking a few questions and even throwing in some feedback. The more she talked, the more she realized how easy he was to talk to. He really listened, he didn't act as if he was in a hurry, and he didn't take over the conversation.

And the more she was around Grant, the more she compared him to her last boyfriend, Brandon. The two men were opposites. Brandon also had a busy schedule with his software start-up, but even when they spent a weekend on vacation together, he'd still been so self-involved, and she'd felt like a decoration at his side.

She and Grant finished discussing upgrades, and the excitement of having her own shop continued to buzz through her. The guests at the Pine Valley ski lodge would find a great variety of gifts in her shop and wouldn't have to rely on packing what they needed for special celebrations. And the items she offered would be more unique and desirable than the gimmicky touristy items.

"Well, one thing at a time, right?" she said, looking over at Grant from where she'd crossed to the storefront window.

"I'm happy to help," he said.

The sincerity in his voice made Maurie's heart do a little flip. "Thanks," she said. "I'll let you know."

She opened the shop door, and Grant went through, then Maurie locked up. When she turned, Grant waited by the truck, holding open the passenger door for her.

"I appreciate your help," Maurie said, approaching the truck, her ankle boots crunching over the windswept snow on the ground.

"No problem." Grant's breath clouded in the cold air, but there wasn't a goose bump in sight.

"How are you not cold?" she asked, pausing next to him.

He shrugged those muscled shoulders of his. "I run hot, I guess."

Yes. Maurie climbed in, and Grant shut her door. Then

Let's Begin Again

she watched him walk around the front of the truck, silently agreeing with him 100 percent.

Seven

When Grant arrived at Maurie's house the next morning, another car was parked in her driveway. It had snowed overnight, and the tire treads from the car were already filled in with white flakes. He assumed the car belonged to Maurie's friend Taffy. When he knocked on the door a minute later, it opened to a blonde woman.

She was a petite woman with a huge smile. "You must be Grant."

"Yes, and you must be Taffy."

She laughed. This woman seemed pretty peppy, if he were to go on his first impression.

"Come on in," she said. "I've got the coffee on." Then she gave him a wink.

Grant wasn't sure exactly how to take her instant friendliness. He'd met this woman all of ten seconds ago.

"Maurie slept in." Taffy continued their one-sided conversation, leading the way into the kitchen. "She'll be out in a minute. She was up half the night looking at those blasted photo albums of her grandparents. I told her not to, but would she listen to me? No. Now she'll be all weepy today."

"Weepy?" Grant felt as if the breath had gone out of him. Should he not have brought the albums down from the attic?

"Well, don't tell her I told *you* anything." Taffy stopped in the middle of the kitchen and turned to survey him. Her scrutiny was quite thorough. "But Maurie has worked really hard to get over her crappy childhood. And I don't want those albums to send her back to that dark place, if you know what I mean?"

She didn't give Grant time to respond but moved to the counter and pulled out mugs from the cupboard. Not that he knew exactly what to say.

"I'm so glad you're renovating this place," Taffy continued. "It looks like a dump, and that can't be good for Maurie's morale either."

Grant opened his mouth to speak, but then the coffee timer went off.

"Perfect." Taffy flashed him a stunning smile over her shoulder.

If Grant were into talkative blondes, he might find her fairly attractive. But he already knew his thoughts were otherwise occupied with a dark-haired lady, if his restless sleep last night was any indication.

Taffy poured the fragrant coffee into the mugs. "Don't tell Maurie, but I made this straight-up black. You can add some sugar or cream if you'd like. Maurie likes to add flavors and other fancy stuff." She waved to a row of bottles lined up on the counter that Grant hadn't seen the day before.

"Black is fine," he said, taking the steaming mug.

Taffy grinned at him in a familiar way that left him wondering if there was some inside joke he was missing.

He took a careful sip of the hot liquid.

Taffy was still watching him. "Well, look at you. All handsome and rugged."

He nearly spat out the sip he'd taken.

"What?" she said in an innocent tone.

Was she flirting, or did she just think he was her instant best friend? He could imagine her working at a trucker's diner, calling everyone "hon" or "sweetheart."

"I'm not sure what you're talking about," he said.

She took a slow sip of her coffee, her gaze locked on him. "I'm sure you know what you look like, Grant Shelton. And you probably have a lot of ladies in your back pocket."

Grant blinked. "Uh." How did one even respond to that? The coffee was suddenly way too bitter. And he was not in the least prepared for this woman's onslaught. He'd lived long enough to know that it needed to stop, now. "Taffy? Can I call you Taffy?"

She fluttered her eyelashes. "Of course."

"Look, I'm not sure what your intentions are, but I can assure you that I'm not a player." He paused. "And we're *not* hooking up."

Taffy's eyes practically bugged out as she raised her brows. And then she burst out laughing.

Grant couldn't move. This was perhaps the strangest and nuttiest woman he'd ever met. She also hadn't spilled a drop of her coffee despite her outburst.

She lifted a finger to point at him, still laughing so hard she could barely speak. Then she finally said, "You're a *gem*, Grant Shelton. You have my one-hundred-and-ten-percent approval."

"Taffy!" A voice came from the hallway. Maurie's.

"Uh-oh." Taffy ran a finger over her lips as if she were zipping them closed. She gave Grant another wink.

Seconds later Maurie joined them in the kitchen. "What are you telling him, Taffy?"

Maurie placed her hands on her hips, and Grant noted

that she looked as if she'd just tumbled out of bed. Not that he was complaining. Her fitted T-shirt had a row of *Z*s on it, stretching across her chest, and her pajama bottoms hung low on her hips, exposing a couple of inches of skin. Definitely not complaining.

"And *what* are you feeding him?" Maurie strode up to Grant, took the mug from him, and sniffed. "Not in my kitchen."

Grant watched in disbelief as she crossed to the kitchen sink and proceeded to pour out the coffee.

"Wait," Grant said. "I was drinking that." What was up with these two women?

Taffy laughed, her gaze zeroing in on Grant. "You're on your own, sugar." She moved past him, trailed her finger along his arm, then sashayed out of the kitchen, still holding her mug. "I'll be in my room, processing orders," she called. "Let me know when lunch is ready."

Taffy paused at the edge of the hallway. "Oh, and Maurie, he's all yours." Then she was gone.

Grant rubbed a hand over his face. What had just happened? Taffy's bedroom door clicked, and seconds later, music began playing.

Slowly, he looked over at Maurie.

"What did she say to you?" Maurie asked, her green eyes completely focused on him.

"What *didn't* she say to me?"

Maurie's eyes widened. "That bad?"

"I don't know if I'd call it *bad*, but certainly educational."

Maurie scoffed, then she picked up the can of instant coffee and dumped it into the trash. "I can only imagine. Just know that Taffy's her own person, and there's no use trying to change her." She said all this with affection in her tone, then she pulled out a bag of roasted coffee beans from the cupboard.

Grant watched her movements for a moment, trying not to ogle her, because he was remembering what Taffy had said about Maurie being weepy.

Maurie didn't seem upset, just . . . underdressed.

"Hey, are you all right?" he asked in a soft voice. "Taffy said you had a rough night."

Maurie stilled, her back toward him. "She said that?"

"Yeah."

Maurie turned. "Sorry about Taffy. She can be a bit . . . transparent."

"That's one way to look at it," Grant said. "But I'm not talking about Taffy. What about *you*?"

Maurie leaned against the counter and looked down at her feet. Grant hadn't seen this side of her, or at least he hadn't for ten years—the quiet girl with a lot on her mind.

"She told you about the albums, didn't she?" Maurie said.

"Yes." He crossed to the counter and leaned against it a couple of feet from her.

Maurie shrugged. "I had a pretty rotten childhood, which you know. But there were good times, too . . . when I was a little kid mostly, although I was too young to remember." She glanced over at him. "Those albums showed me what might have been, I suppose. If my grandparents had lived longer and my mom hadn't gone off the deep end."

"Maurie, look, I'm really sorry," he started. "I—"

She held up a hand. "It's all in the past, and—" Her voice cut off. And when she spoke again, it was trembling. "I've been lucky in many ways, but I wish that my dad hadn't left and that my mom could have been stronger." Tears rolled down her cheeks, and she closed her eyes.

"Hey," he said in a soft voice. He closed the distance between them and pulled her into his arms. She rested her head against his chest as if it was the most natural thing in the world. And Grant had to admit that she fit there perfectly.

He hated that she was hurting so much. And he hated that there was nothing he could do to fix it. Maurie wasn't like a house that could be fixed up with a hammer and nails. Grant rubbed her back as she sniffled. After a moment, he became aware of other things about Maurie. The warmth of her skin, the tickle of her hair against his chin, the flutter of her pulse. And although she'd just woken up, she smelled sweet, like chocolate and peppermint… Perhaps she'd had her gourmet hot chocolate this morning already.

The thought made him smile.

Her breathing steadied, and her trembling subsided. He started to relax more because she was relaxing. He felt the change in her body as she took a few deep, calming breaths. His own temperature had warmed up considerably where they'd touched, and his heart was beating a steady thud.

He should release her. Soon. Her smell and her touch were intoxicating, and his mind was wandering way off course. Space between them would be good. Inch by inch, they separated, but she kept her hands at his waist when she looked up at him, her smile tremulous. "Thanks," she whispered.

Grant gazed into her green eyes, her lashes damp with tears. They were only inches apart, yet he craved to be closer again. He hadn't wanted their embrace to end, which was ridiculous, because he hardly knew Maurie. Just because she was in distress and had let him hold her, that didn't mean that there was something more between them. While he talked himself out of pulling her into his arms again, he realized he *did* know Maurie. More than he should admit. And none of his current thoughts were exactly platonic.

"Thanks for listening, Grant. You're a good man." She lifted up on her toes and kissed him on the cheek.

Her scent swept over him again, and his skin tingled where she'd pressed her warm mouth.

"Maurie," he said, grasping her hand to stop her from pulling away too soon.

She stilled, her gaze meeting his. Her breathing seemed rapid, and he couldn't help but focus on her parted lips.

"I always wondered what happened to you over the years," he said.

She seemed to move a fraction closer, or was that his imagination? Her fingers threaded through his, and a warm shiver spread up his arm.

"I wondered about you too," she said softly, almost a whisper. She'd stopped crying, but her eyes were luminescent with her tears. "I had a huge crush on you."

When she smiled, Grant smiled back. His heart sounded like a freight train in his ears. He had to tell her. He couldn't stand her gazing at him as if he was some sort of nice guy. She had to know the truth about her last night in Pine Valley.

"Maurie, I always wanted to get to know you better," he said. "Being a teenager was complicated, and you were like a shadow who came and went. Sometimes I hoped when I did yard work at your house that you'd come out and talk to me."

Her eyes widened. "You did?"

He chuckled. "Of course. I'd wait for your mom to leave, and then I'd come over. For some reason I couldn't bring myself to knock on your door and talk to you." This was it; the time was now. "Maurie, I need to—"

She stopped him.

Maurie wrapped her arms around his neck, then she pressed her mouth against his and kissed him. Sensation burst through him, and Grant forgot all reservations. He cradled her face with his hands, angling his mouth over hers. She tasted sweet, just as he knew she would.

Maurie's fingers moved into his hair, and she kissed him with unexpected depth and passion, as if she'd been waiting to kiss him for a while. He knew he had been waiting to kiss her. The music coming from the back bedroom echoed the rhythm of his hammering heart.

Grant backed her up against the counter and continued to kiss her, taking the lead. Maurie practically melted into him. Her hands were in his hair, then on his shoulders, then clutching at his shirt.

He had to slow things down. Right now.

He broke off their kissing. "Wow," he said, leaning his forehead against hers, trying to calm his breathing.

Her eyes were still closed. "Yeah, wow," she whispered.

Grant didn't want to release her. He wanted more. But it wasn't the right time or place or . . . "I think I need to get to work," he said.

She opened her eyes, and he saw something akin to happiness there. So much better than her tears.

"Too hot in the kitchen?" she asked with a half smile.

"Yeah." He traced his fingers along her jaw, and she closed her eyes again. "Mind if I open a couple of windows?"

Maurie nodded.

"Okay." He leaned down again and kissed her lightly on the mouth. "Dinner tonight?"

"Sure."

"With*out* Taffy?"

"Hey, she's my friend." Maurie slid her hands down his arms, then squeezed his hands before letting him go. "Dinner sounds great."

Eight

Maurie rubbed the too-dark lip gloss from her lips. She didn't want to look like she was trying too hard. She was still reeling from the fact that she'd kissed Grant and that he'd kissed her back. Maurie gazed at her reflection in the bathroom mirror. Nothing had changed about her, yet she felt different inside. A hope was growing, one that was foreign. Perhaps it was because Grant had always been the best memory of her past, and now they'd crossed that line of friends to . . . what?

She didn't know. But the thought of Grant, the way he looked at her, and the way he'd kissed her, made her stomach twinge. And now she was getting ready for her dinner date with Grant. He'd gone home to shower and change, and she felt as if she'd been floating ever since.

Maurie touched her neck, remembering her adventure in the kitchen with Grant. Heat stole along her skin. She hadn't told Taffy about the kiss, or kisses, at least not yet.

Taffy had made no secret of Maurie liking Grant, but when it came down to it, it had only been a couple of months since Maurie's breakup with Brandon. Was she on the rebound? What did Grant truly think about her? Would he break her heart? Hearts weren't breakable if they were carefully guarded, right?

A knock sounded at the front door as Maurie examined her collection of lip glosses.

Taffy passed the bathroom. "I'll get the door."

Maurie picked up a pale-pink gloss and applied it. There, that looked better. She stepped back from the mirror and surveyed her appearance. Her long, black sweater over dark-gray leggings wasn't too casual or too dressy. She was also wearing her black ankle boots with two-inch heels. Grant was tall enough that she'd still be shorter than him. She'd chosen her pearl earrings and pearl-drop necklace, inherited from her foster mom.

Taffy's laughter streamed from the front room, and Maurie took a couple of deep breaths. Would their meeting be awkward? Friendly?

She couldn't stall forever. So she exited the bathroom and turned the corner to the living room. Maurie slowed her steps, stunned.

She'd seen Grant only in work clothing so far, which had been pleasing enough. But now that he was dressed up, Maurie wondered how this guy had stayed single for so long after his divorce. He'd shaved, and he wore dark slacks with a black leather jacket over a pale-blue, button-down shirt that was open at the collar. The blue of his shirt made his eyes a deeper blue. His brown hair looked slightly damp, and as she neared him, his cologne became distinct.

"Hi," he said in a low voice, his gaze soaking her in, from her hair waving about her shoulders, down the length of her body.

When their gazes met again, she only saw appreciation in his, and her pulse thrummed to life. "Hi," she said.

"All righty then," Taffy said, her voice laced with laughter. "It looks like you two are ready to go. Have a great time. And don't worry about me here alone. There's a new series I want to binge-watch on Netflix."

Maurie turned to Taffy. "Do you want me to bring you something back?"

"Ah, no." Taffy winked. "I'm not so fond of leftovers. This will give me a chance to eat some of the contraband food I snuck into your house."

"Funny." Maurie hugged her friend. "We won't be too late."

"I'm still not planning on staying up," Taffy said.

Maurie was really glad she hadn't told Taffy about the kiss. Otherwise, her friend would probably be teasing her more. As it was, Taffy practically pushed Maurie and Grant out the door. Maurie stopped on the porch when she saw the crossover SUV parked in the driveway.

"No truck?" she asked.

"I wasn't going to bring my work truck on a date." Grant slipped his hand into hers, a question in his gaze.

A thrill ran through her at his touch. The affectionate gesture told her so much: that he remembered their kiss as well and that he was definitely interested in her. She smiled at him, and he linked their fingers, then led her down the steps and along the icy walkway to the driveway.

"I'm not complaining," she said.

He chuckled and opened the passenger door. She climbed in, finding the interior warm. She leaned against the seat and released a sigh as he walked around the front.

When he climbed in, she asked, "Any FaceTiming with Trent tonight?"

"Yeah, actually," Grant said as he started the engine. He backed out of the driveway. "Trent's been sending me selfies like crazy too. I might have created a monster."

After he straightened out the wheel of the car, he handed her his phone. "Here, look at the texts he sent."

She took the phone and opened the discussion labeled "Trent" and laughed when she saw the pictures of the different expressions of a little boy who looked like a mini-me of Grant. "Wow, he looks so much like you."

"That's what everyone says," he said. "The good news is that it means I'm his real father."

"What do you mean?" she asked with a sinking heart.

Grant turned the next corner, heading toward Main Street. "Joy believed in sharing her love with more than her husband."

"That's rough." Maurie felt awful for him, and she was having a hard time imagining a woman who wouldn't find satisfaction with one man, especially a man like Grant. "How long were you married?"

"About a year." Grant blew out a breath. "Most of it was pretty miserable. But Joy was pregnant, and I tried to stick it out for the kid. I had a hard time believing the child was mine, until he was born, that is."

Maurie heard the pain and frustration in his voice when he talked about Joy, but love when he spoke about Trent.

"Well, your son's adorable," Maurie said, scrolling through the last of the pictures. Trent looked like a happy, healthy boy. When she finished with the pictures, she set the phone in the middle console. "What does he like to do?"

"He's pretty much obsessed with all reptiles and dinosaurs," Grant said, his tone warm. "I can't even pronounce half of the dinosaur names he knows. His brain is like a sponge."

"Kids are remarkable," Maurie said.

Grant nodded. "Despite all the crap that's gone on with Joy, I wouldn't trade my son for anything."

They fell into silence for few minutes, but it was a comfortable silence. Maurie admired his profile. In it she saw determination and resilience. And, most of all, loyalty.

Grant slowed the truck at a stop light. "Maybe someday you'll meet Trent."

A thrill ran through Maurie at the suggestion because it was clear Trent held most of Grant's heart. "I'd love that."

He flashed her a smile, his blue eyes holding hers for a few seconds before he refocused on driving. "We'll have to arrange it then."

His answer made her heart flutter. She wasn't sure when spring break was, when he said he'd have his son for a visit. But if Grant and she were still friends—still dating—that sounded perfectly fine to her.

"Where are we going?" she asked as he turned onto the canyon road that led to the ski resorts and mountain slopes.

"The lodge restaurant has a great menu. Have you been there before?"

She laughed. "No."

Grant glanced at her. "Never?"

"Hardly," Maurie said. "I pretty much ate out of cans and boxes growing up. My mom wasn't much of a cook. It wasn't until I moved into foster care that my eyes were opened to the heaven that good food can bring."

"Good food *is* heaven," he said with a smile as he pulled off a turn in the road. "I don't know if the food will be as great as your foster mom's, but it's the best Pine Valley has to offer." He continued to drive toward a large lodge blazing with lights. He slowed as he drove through the parking lot.

"Sounds great to me."

Grant pulled into a parking space, but instead of shutting off the ignition, he asked in a quiet voice, "Was it hard? Leaving Pine Valley and everything you knew?"

It was a complicated question with an even more complicated answer. Maurie had been over this a few times with her therapist when Maurie realized she'd been grieving losing her childhood, her mother, and everything she'd been used to—no matter how dysfunctional it had been.

"Yes, it was hard," Maurie said, her own voice quiet. "But I learned to make the best of my future."

Grant gazed at her, and Maurie wished she could know what was going through his mind. "It wasn't like I could be more miserable than I already was." She took a deep breath. "Honestly, the only thing I missed was you."

One of Grant's brows arched. And then the edges of his mouth lifted in a mischievous quirk.

"Don't let it go to your head, okay?" she clarified.

Grant was smiling now.

She puffed out a breath. "I mean, yeah, I did have a crush on you, but the things you did around our yard also gave me a sense of comfort."

"It wasn't my good looks?" He waggled his brows.

Maurie laughed. "That might have been part of it."

Grant reached across the space that divided them and grasped her hand. "I hated that you had to leave."

His words made her legs feel like water.

"Thanks," she whispered, and he squeezed her hand. "You were always watching out for me. And even though we barely spoke to each other, you saw me for who I was."

"I asked around to find out where you'd gone," Grant said. "But no one would tell me anything."

Maurie stared at him. He'd *looked* for her? "Child Protective Services is like that."

"There were a lot of rumors," Grant said. "And I guess I worried—"

"You didn't need to worry," she said. "After a few weeks

in foster care, I realized how messed up my life had been, and I felt lucky to have escaped when I did."

"Truly?" His gaze was intense.

"Yes, truly." She was surprised at his intensity, as if he somehow felt responsible for her happiness.

"So . . ." he said, amusement replacing the intensity. "You had a pretty big crush on me, huh?"

"I think I already made that clear."

"Hmm." He leaned toward her. "I think I had a crush on you too."

Her pulse fluttered at his words, then soared as he lifted his free hand and ran his thumb along her jaw. Grant kissed her slowly, as if he was savoring each second.

Maurie couldn't help but melt against him. She slid her hands around his neck, the warmth of his skin sending goose bumps skittering along her own arms, and kissed him back. Maybe they could stay in his SUV and keep kissing instead of going into a public restaurant. But her growling stomach betrayed her.

Grant drew away with a chuckle. "Hungry?"

"Don't stop," she whispered, not releasing him.

He pressed his mouth against hers, but briefly this time. "I'm glad you came home, Maurie Ledbetter."

"Me too, Grant Shelton." Perhaps she wouldn't have chosen the events that had separated her from Grant, but she was grateful to be here. Now.

"We're going to be late for our reservation," Grant murmured, his fingers tracing her jaw again, then moving down her neck.

"Okay, okay," she said. She felt like she was going to ignite if he kept touching her like this. She playfully shoved him away.

Grant grinned, then popped open his door and climbed out.

While he walked around the SUV to open her door, Maurie marveled at what he'd told her. To think that all those years ago, Grant had noticed her, had cared about her, had worried about her. It was amazing to comprehend.

When Grant opened her door, she climbed out and linked her fingers with his. Their touching was becoming more and more natural. She decided she could get used to being with Grant really fast.

They walked to the lodge, which looked like a winter wonderland from the outside. The Christmas decorations had been transformed into valentines. Pine trees on display at the entrance had been wrapped in gauze plus silver and pink hearts.

It reminded her that Valentine's Day would be coming up in a couple of weeks, right around her planned opening of her store. She'd have to capitalize on that with her promotions.

Grant opened the lodge door, and Maurie stepped inside the beautiful building. Even the rustic wood pillars looked elegant. And the smell of the restaurant area was divine—some sort of baked cinnamon.

Grant led her by the hand toward the hostess stand.

A dark-haired woman smiled at their approach. Her nametag identified her as *Alicia*.

"Grant?" Alicia said.

"Oh, hi," Grant said, his tone friendly. "You work here now?"

"Keeping busy." She gave him an exaggerated wink.

Maurie wasn't sure how to take the gesture. With Taffy, it would have been all in fun. But Maurie didn't know Alicia.

Alicia leaned forward on the podium and clasped her hands together as if she had all the time in the world. "How's business going for you?"

"Keeping busy too," Grant said. "And trying to fit in time with Trent."

Alicia smiled. "He's such a sweetheart."

Maurie's stomach churned. This beautiful, sophisticated woman knew Grant well enough for him to discuss his son with her.

Grant laughed. "He can be. I wish I could spend more time with him."

"Of course you do," Alicia practically cooed. She glanced at Maurie and gave her the briefest of smiles. "Two of you?"

"Yes, there should be a reservation," he said.

"Right. There you are." Alicia looked up, a bright smile on her face. "Gwen will take care of you."

As if the waitress named Gwen had been listening in, she suddenly appeared.

Maurie studied the waitress. Long, blonde hair. Flawless makeup. Beauty must be a requirement to work at this restaurant.

"Hi, Grant," Gwen said.

Maurie tried not to scoff. It seemed that Grant knew plenty of women in Pine Valley. And why shouldn't he? He'd lived here his whole life. Of course, now Maurie was wondering how many of these women he'd dated . . . before he married Joy, that was, since he'd said he hadn't dated much since his divorce.

Gwen led them to a booth, and Maurie slid into one side, and Grant took the other. Maurie tried not to let the waitress's familiar banter with Grant bother her.

"Looks like it's busy tonight," Grant said smoothly, as if the woman's megawatt smile had no effect on him.

"Yeah, Fridays are usually like that." Gwen smiled and glanced at Maurie. "What drinks can I start you with?"

Maybe Maurie was being overly sensitive, because Gwen

was equally friendly with her. "I'll have water with lemon, no ice," Maurie said.

Grant's brows lifted just a bit.

After he ordered, Gwen left their table with her smile still in place.

Maurie leaned forward. "You've got a lot of lady friends here. Were you in high school together?"

Grant's blue eyes met hers. "Alicia left Pine Valley soon after she graduated. I'm not sure about Gwen; I don't think she's been in Pine Valley long."

Maurie nodded, feeling a pebble in her throat.

"Maurie," Grant said, amusement in his tone. "None of them is as interesting as you."

Warmth traveled up her neck, and she looked down at her hands. "I'm not fishing for a compliment."

"I know you're not." His voice was low. "But know that I'm on a date with *you*, not any other woman."

She met his gaze, and the warmth continued into her cheeks. She was acting like a jealous . . . girlfriend. She had no claim on Grant. They'd shared a couple of kisses, and this was their first date. "Have you dated either of them?"

Grant's gaze didn't waver. "No."

And Maurie believed him, but she still had questions. She couldn't very well drill Grant on his former love life right now though.

"Maurie . . ." Grant was still watching her.

She swallowed. "I haven't been on a date in a while. So I'm probably messing stuff up. I don't need to know your dating history."

Grant didn't seem annoyed, but he'd have every right to be. "I don't know Alicia too well, but Gwen's just flirty. With me, with everyone, from what I've seen."

Maurie nodded.

"What about you?" he asked. "Are there any men in your Pine Valley past?"

She laughed. "You know there aren't... except, well, you."

Grant grinned. "Good to hear. I don't want to have to get into a fight in a restaurant."

"Ha. Ha." Maurie smirked.

"Believe me, one of the cruxes of being single and in a small town—everyone knows you're available." He paused. "So, uh, after tonight, there might be rumors going around."

"About us?"

Grant shrugged, but he was smiling again. And that smile was making all her parts feel melty again.

Nine

Grant sort of liked the jealous side of Maurie. He found it rather endearing. And yes, they hadn't really dated yet, and things were so new, but Grant hadn't missed how Maurie had sized up Alicia and Gwen.

Gwen reappeared, an order pad in hand. "Had a chance to look at the menu?"

Not at all, Grant wanted to say. But he knew what he wanted. He looked at Maurie, who browsed the menu quickly, then said, "I'll take the salmon salad."

"Great choice," Gwen said in a friendly tone.

Grant made a quick scan of Gwen. Petite, blonde, spunky. Then his gaze shifted to Maurie. Her dark hair, green eyes, and taller and curvier form were more attractive to Grant. But it wasn't just her appearance; it was her depth, her fortitude that attracted him. Not to mention the way she looked at him.

And . . . he should probably look at the menu. "I'll take the top sirloin."

"Excellent," Gwen said, flashing a smile. "I'll bring out some fresh rolls right away."

Grant watched Maurie as she watched Gwen walk away. And Grant could see that her worries hadn't fully dissipated. He wondered what sort of relationships she'd had with men. Had she been through any boyfriends? Casually dated? Been serious with anyone?

"So, where did you go to college?" Grant asked, because he didn't want to ask his other questions in a public restaurant. And the more he knew about how fine and normal Maurie's life had been, the less he had to feel guilty about.

Maurie told him about college and what had led to her gift-basket retailer idea.

"What about you?" she asked.

"Community college," Grant said. "I pretty much knew I wanted to be in construction, so I decided to get an associate's degree in business and learn some of the behind-the-scenes stuff."

"Makes sense," she said. "Is that when you met Joy?"

"Yeah," Grant said. She'd pretty much whirled into his life like a tornado, and before he knew it, they were an item. And she was pregnant. "I'd dated some in high school, but Joy was my first girlfriend. She was pretty intense, but I didn't know better."

Maurie took a sip of her water, and he liked how she seemed to be paying attention to only him. Listening to every word. Joy always had multiple things going at once, whether it was texting or emails or changing the subject over and over.

"So you got married and had Trent," Maurie said in a thoughtful tone. "Were things good for a while at least?"

"I thought so," Grant said. "As long as I was Mr. Obedient Husband. And she could do whatever *she* wanted."

Maurie winced. "Well, I'm glad you're free now. From her."

She was blushing, and Grant smiled. "Me too."

Gwen appeared with the rolls, smiled, and left.

Grant picked up a warm roll from the plate and broke it open, then slathered it with what looked like honey butter. He took a bite. Yep, it was.

Maurie prepared her roll too and took a bite.

"What about you, Maurie?" he asked. "Any heartbreakers in your past?"

She wiped her mouth with a napkin, then took a drink. "No dating in high school. I'm sure you're not surprised."

Before he could refute her statement, she said, "I was an awkward person for a long time. College was like a new beginning. I was finally an adult, and I liked being treated as an adult. I went out a little, but it took a while to feel like I was a normal girl on a normal date."

Grant nodded and ate more of his roll, waiting for her to continue.

"Brandon was my first boyfriend," she said. "We broke up a couple of months ago."

Grant was curious about her tone. Hurt? Regretful? "What was Brandon like?"

"Well, he wasn't a player, so that was good," Maurie said. "But he was . . . sort of self-involved, is the best way to put it." She shrugged. "He ran a start-up software company that kept him really busy. I was impressed with his entrepreneurship. But I soon found out that he wasn't really interested in *me*. It was more like he wanted someone to attend social functions with him."

Grant frowned. "I find it hard to believe that he wasn't interested in you."

Maurie shrugged. "As long as things revolved around *him*, things were good."

"Ah," Grant said. "Sort of the feeling of always being left to hold the wet, dripping coat at a party?"

One side of her mouth lifted. "Exactly." She held his gaze, and Grant knew he was in danger of getting lost in those green eyes of hers.

Gwen appeared at their table, carrying their dinner plates. She set them down, then said, "Anything else I can get either of you?"

When Maurie said no, Gwen left.

They took the first bites of their food, then Maurie turned the questioning on him. "Did you always want to strike out on your own?"

"I was much happier doing certain jobs than others," he said, cutting another piece of steak. "Working with a large construction company meant I always had to listen to the boss before I could make decisions and dive into a job."

"And now?" she asked.

"Now I have to listen to my sister, Julie, since she does the scheduling."

Maurie laughed. Then she sobered. "How many siblings do you have? I realize I've never heard about your family."

Grant finished eating the bite of steak he'd just taken. "One sister, who's married to Dave Briggs," he said. "Thus the Briggs Brothers name of our company. My parents sold their house and bought a condo in a new development on the other side of town."

"Does your sister have kids?" Maurie asked.

"Two."

Maurie nodded. "So she works part-time from the house?"

"Yeah, her job's pretty flexible."

"I think it's great that she can do both," Maurie said. "Raise kids and have something to call her own."

"Is that what you want to do someday?" he asked. "Keep your store going even if you have a family?"

"I can always hire someone to work in the store," Maurie said. "So it would definitely be possible. There's a lot of things that don't require face-to-face interaction. You know, so if a kid's crying, it's not like I can't take a break."

Grant didn't miss the flush of her cheeks. He cut into his steak and took another bite. He couldn't remember a first date where so many serious topics were discussed.

"Well, I can't complain about my current situation," he said. "I make more money now, and I have more flexibility. I can set my own schedule and take off holidays if I want to. That's especially important when Trent's with me."

Maurie didn't seem put off when he talked about Trent, and Grant liked that about her.

"Do you ever take Trent on jobs with you?" Maurie asked.

Grant chuckled. "Um . . . no. He's way too much of a busybody and asks endless questions. Besides, he loves to play with his cousins when he's in Pine Valley. But mostly, I work my schedule around his."

"You're a great dad, Grant," she said in a soft voice.

Something in his heart pulled. Maurie never talked about her dad—who'd abandoned the family, and as far as he knew, hadn't been heard from again. So the wistfulness in her eyes made Grant all the more determined to be a good dad to his son, no matter the miles that separated them.

Gwen returned. "How was everything?"

Grant had finished his meal, but Maurie had only eaten about half of her salad.

"Want any dessert?" Gwen said. "To-go boxes?"

"I'm full," Maurie said. "But I'd love a to-go box."

Gwen nodded, then looked over at Grant. "And you?"

"No dessert for me, thanks," he said. "I'll take the bill."

Gwen smiled and set the bill folder on the table. "Have a great evening. Thanks for coming in."

"Here you go," Grant said before Gwen could leave. He handed over the bill folder with his credit card inside.

"Be back in a minute," Gwen said.

Before Grant could resume his conversation with Maurie, a man approached their table, carrying a plate of what looked like a giant slice of chocolate cake. "Hello, folks," he said. "I'm Seth Owens, the owner of the restaurant. How did you enjoy your meals?"

"Mine was great," Maurie said, eyeing the chocolate cake.

Seth Owens smiled. "Nice to hear. And you, sir?"

"The steak was very good," Grant said.

Seth placed the dessert on the table, then produced two forks. "I've brought a complimentary dessert for you to try. All that we ask is that you rate it on our website. If you're too full now, we can box it up."

But Maurie reached for a fork. "What kind of cake?"

"Chocolate raspberry, with a little something special." Seth moved a step back. "Enjoy."

"Thank you," Grant said. He turned to look at Maurie, who'd speared a bite of chocolate cake and a raspberry on her fork.

She lifted a brow, then put the cake in her mouth. "Oh, that's good."

"I guess we're eating dessert then?"

Maurie smiled. "Can't beat free," she said and dug in.

Grant tried the cake. The chocolatey goodness was rich and creamy. "Wow, it is good." He speared another piece. It was kind of fun sharing the cake with Maurie. And he didn't mind watching her enjoy it either. "Not as good as your cinnamon rolls though."

Maurie laughed. "You're a charmer, Grant Shelton."

"I'll take that as a compliment, Maurie Ledbetter."

She shook her head and ate more cake. "Okay, I'm really stuffed now. You're going to have to roll me to the car."

"Maybe we can work it off this weekend," Grant said. "Have you ever been skiing?"

By the look on her face, Grant knew the answer was no.

"I'm pretty swamped right now," she said, "and I'm not all that coordinated."

Grant tilted his head. "You've never been?"

A blush stole across her cheeks, and she shook her head.

"We can stay on the bunny hill."

Her brows shot up.

"You know, the easy slope for the beginners," he said.

"I don't think so," Maurie said, glancing away. "I mean, I'm going to embarrass you."

"Not possible," Grant said.

She arched a brow. "How do you know?"

"I just know," he said. "Being with you is different. You're . . . I don't know how to explain it."

She narrowed those beautiful green eyes of hers. "Is 'different' good or bad?"

"Oh, definitely good," he said with a smile.

And there it was. Another blush.

Ten

"To paint or not to paint?" Maurie muttered as she scrolled through Pinterest and lounged on her bed.

"Did I hear the word paint?" Taffy asked, coming into Maurie's bedroom.

Somewhere in the house, a drill was buzzing. Grant was hard at work as usual. In the three days he'd been working on her place, the transformation was already noticeable.

Maurie angled her laptop screen to show Taffy. "What do you think about a robin's-egg blue for the trim work inside the shop?"

Taffy sat on the edge of the bed and considered the Pinterest image that was of a cozy café somewhere in Seattle. Maurie loved the blues and yellows of the café.

"I love it," Taffy pronounced. She folded her arms. "There's also a lonely man out there. What did you do to him?"

Maurie sat up. "What do you mean? What did *I* do to him?"

Taffy narrowed her eyes. "You said your date the other

night was wonderful, yet you're always in here or at the shop when he's over. Go in there and talk to him, girl. That hunk of a man will not remain single for long."

Exhaling, Maurie rubbed her forehead.

Taffy touched her arm. "What's wrong? Was he a jerk, and you didn't want to say something?"

Maurie dropped her hand. "No, nothing like that. In fact, he's the complete opposite. He asked me to go skiing, and well, I guess I'm sort of avoiding telling him no."

"I don't get it . . ."

"It's dumb, really," Maurie said.

"Tell me," Taffy said. "I'm sure it's not dumb. Besides, you know I'm going to get it out of you anyway."

"Right," Maurie said with a small smile. "It's just that . . . when I lived in Pine Valley, I watched all the other kids do stuff that I couldn't do, or my mom wouldn't let me do. I used to tell myself those things weren't fun anyway. They were boring or dangerous. Skiing or sledding would be too freezing to try. I didn't have a winter coat, let alone snow boots. Hot chocolate at the gas station was gross. The school dances were lame. Hiking and picnics with other teens would be too awkward. And that I could never afford a cute enough swimsuit to go swimming in the lakes."

"Oh, hon," Taffy said.

Maurie's eyes burned. "My therapist told me it was my coping skill." She shrugged. "If I go skiing and find that I love it and that it's not boring, then . . ."

Taffy nodded. "Then you'll realize what you really did miss out on as a kid."

Throat tight, Maurie said, "Exactly."

Taffy pulled Maurie into a hug. Maurie closed her eyes and kept her breathing calm and even. It was a trick her therapist had taught her. When things and memories or regrets seemed too overwhelming, she should focus instead on simply breathing.

When Taffy pulled away, her eyes were moist. "Here's the thing," Taffy said. "When you're forty, you'll look back on your twenties and thirties and regret not doing things *now*."

Maurie frowned. "What do you mean?"

"You've got a hot man in your living room who's been through a lot of crap too," Taffy said in a hushed voice. "Not as much as you, of course, but crap nonetheless. Go skiing with him. Have fun. Do it for that sad little girl who used to live in this house. Show her you're strong and it's never too late to live out dreams. Maybe you'll hate skiing, or you'll love it. Doesn't matter. At least you're living. You're the new Maurie. And adding Grant Shelton into the mix isn't a bad idea either."

Maurie blinked against the stinging in her eyes. "You should be a therapist."

Taffy burst out laughing, and Maurie joined in. Then their laughter faded, and Taffy nudged Maurie. "There's a man in our house."

Maurie snickered. "I get it. I get it." She closed her laptop and climbed off her bed. Leaving Taffy behind, Maurie walked into the hallway. The drilling had stopped, and the front door opened and shut.

Had Grant left?

Maurie moved to the living room and peered out the window. Grant's truck was still in front of the house, and he was sorting through a box or something in the bed of his truck.

He straightened and turned, then headed toward the house. Maurie moved out of the line of vision from the window so he wouldn't see her watching him.

She entered the kitchen just as the front door opened. Turning to see him, she tried to act casual. "Hi."

Grant shut the door, then looked over at her. "Hey."

His blue gaze connected with hers, and a warm shiver traveled along her arms.

"How's it going?" she asked, a bit lamely.

His mouth quirked, but he didn't laugh. "Excellent. Want to see the hallway closet?"

"Sure." Did she sound breathless? She felt breathless.

Grant led the way to the hall closet, as if she needed to be guided. He'd replaced the door yesterday, but she hadn't looked inside yet.

He opened the door, and Maurie gazed at the repaired wall, new shelf, and rod. With the new doorframe and door, the closet looked brand new. "All that's left is the paint and carpet."

"I like painting," Taffy said, appearing in the hallway.

Grant smiled over at her. "You'll have to ask the boss." Then he winked at Maurie.

Taffy walked toward them, then paused in front of the closet, standing on the left side of Maurie so that she had to step back, which put her closer to Grant.

She didn't know how he managed to stay smelling nice throughout his long workdays.

"I love it," Taffy said. "You do nice work, Grant."

"Thank you." His deep voice rumbled in the stillness.

"Well, back to work," Taffy said in a singsong voice, casting a *talk-to-him* glare at Maurie. Then Taffy headed down the hall and shut the door to her bedroom. Seconds later, music started to boom.

Maurie took a step away from Grant, putting some distance between them. "I agree with Taffy," she said, her voice sounding all trembly and nervous. "You do nice work."

Grant rested a hand on the doorframe and nodded. His blue eyes were intent on hers, and Maurie knew he hadn't missed the nervous pitch in her voice. He was a detail-oriented construction worker, after all.

"Have you been avoiding me, Maurie?" he asked in a low voice.

Her insides felt mushy, and her throat tight. "I've been really busy, Grant, you know with the store and all."

He nodded. And waited.

Maurie puffed out a breath. "I haven't been avoiding you, at least not purposely."

One of his brows lifted. He wasn't buying it.

"All right." She shoved her hands into her jeans pockets because they were sort of trembling. "I will go skiing with you."

Surprise flashed across Grant's face, and he straightened. "Really?"

A lightness bubbled through Maurie. "Really. I'll make a total fool of myself, and you'll get plenty of entertainment, but I'll go." She paused a heartbeat. "With you."

Grant's smile was slow. Warm.

And then he moved toward her. He was getting close, so close.

Maurie backed up, but she only bumped into the wall.

Grant rested a hand on the wall, inches from her head. He smelled of clean soap and a little spice. "I'm glad you changed your mind."

"I didn't exactly say no," Maurie said.

Grant's gaze dropped to her mouth. "I figured the avoiding me thing meant you didn't want to go. You could have said *no*. Plain and simple."

"I could have," Maurie said. "Sometimes things are complicated." Her pulse was acting wild, and she was sure that Grant could hear her heart pounding. He wasn't even touching her, yet she felt the warmth of his skin against hers.

"Skiing doesn't have to be complicated," Grant said.

Maurie exhaled. "Stop looking at me like that."

"Like what?"

"Like you want to kiss me."

Grant's lips curved. "I do want to kiss you."

Maurie was pretty sure she was blushing furiously. And then he did kiss her. Maurie grasped the fabric of his shirt and dragged him closer. He came willingly, pressing against her, until she was pinned between the wall and his body. Not that she minded. It was quite heavenly.

His mouth explored hers, slow and deliberate, as if he'd been wanting to kiss her, but he was also aware that Taffy was still in the house.

Maurie breathed in everything that was Grant Shelton. His scent, his warm skin, the stubble along his jaw, the way his hands gripped her hips and didn't seem to be letting go anytime soon.

"Grant," she whispered against his mouth. "You must really like skiing."

He chuckled, his chest rumbling against hers. And then he kissed her jawline ever so slowly, trailing kisses and creating a path of fire to her neck.

"I should . . . get back to work," Maurie said, placing her hand against his chest. His firm, muscled chest. "And so should you."

Grant smiled against her neck. "Is that an order, boss?"

"It is."

He kissed her neck, then lifted his head. His eyes were even bluer than she remembered. "Tomorrow?"

"I don't have any, uh, ski equipment."

Grant released her then stepped back. He scanned her from head to foot. "You can borrow my sister's stuff. It should fit."

"I don't want to put her out—" Maurie started, but Grant cut her off with a stern look.

"We'll go around four and get in a couple of hours before it's dark," he said. "It will be less crowded."

Maurie swallowed. "Okay." She missed the warmth of Grant's body, but she couldn't continue to maul him in the hallway. At least not with only two inches of wood separating them from Taffy.

Grant grasped her hand and squeezed. "It will be fun," he said. "And if you get too cold, the lodge has hot chocolate. I mean, hot *cocoa*."

The lump in her throat was the size of Texas. "As long as your sister doesn't mind."

"She won't," Grant said. "I'll bring over the stuff in the morning, and you can try it all on."

"Sounds good." For a second, Maurie thought he might kiss her again. But he released her hand and stepped away. Was it terrible for her to want him to kiss her again? To not want to let him go? *Don't get so attached,* she told herself. Breaking things off with Brandon had been hard enough. She'd learned a lot about herself, about how to keep her identity separate from another person's. Grant Shelton was pretty amazing, but like Taffy said, he had his own crap.

"I'm going to get that light fixture replaced," Grant said, looking back into the closet.

Apparently he was being very obedient and getting back to work.

Eleven

"Isn't Maurie our customer?" Julie asked Grant, her hands on her hips, as they stood in front of the hallway closet, where she kept her ski clothing.

"She is," Grant said, not giving more than an inch of information. Julie would read into his request to borrow her ski clothing enough as it was.

"And you're . . . going skiing together?"

"We are." Again Grant didn't elaborate. Julie had set him up a few months ago with a perfectly awful blind date who would have put Godzilla's bride to shame.

Julie blinked, then she tilted her head. "Was this your idea—"

"Sis," Grant interrupted. "Can we skip the Twenty Questions? I'm tired."

At this, Julie's brows pulled together. "Are you okay?"

Her tone was loaded with more than a single question.

"Joy and I got into an argument last night," he said. "She says that my phone calls, or more accurately my FaceTiming with Trent each night, gets him too wound up for bed. It takes him over an hour to fall asleep after."

Julie nodded. She was well-versed in the Joy drama. "Call him earlier then."

"That's what I offered," Grant said with a sigh. "But you know Joy. She has every minute of his day and night scheduled. When can a kid just be a kid?"

As if on cue, Julie's son, Riley—who was a year older than Trent—let out a bloodcurdling scream. Julie didn't even flinch.

"Is he okay?" Grant said.

"I set the Wi-Fi to kick off after an hour of his video gaming." She shrugged.

Riley's screaming had stopped, so Grant figured it wasn't fatal.

Julie pulled out a white-and-blue ski jacket, then handed it to Grant. "How tall is she?"

"A couple of inches shorter than you."

Next, Julie handed him light-blue ski pants, then a beanie and a pair of warm ski gloves. "She'll want to layer. Do you want my skis and boots too?"

"We'll rent," Grant said. "I'm not sure what her shoe size is."

Julie met his gaze.

Grant knew that look in her eyes. She still had questions, but she was using major control not to pester him.

"Okay, well, have fun," Julie said.

"Mo-om!" her son called, his voice that whiney tone only a parent could tolerate.

"Shoo," Julie said. "If he sees you, he'll never let you leave."

Grant chuckled softly. "Thanks for this."

Julie nodded and folded her arms. "You know I want a full report."

"Okay, *Mom*, we'll see." Grant winked, then gave his

sister a quick hug. She'd always been in his corner. Through the divorce and generously helping with Trent.

Grant left Julie's, then drove over to Maurie's house. Her car was gone when he pulled up, and he wondered if she was at her store, painting. He'd heard her discuss colors with Taffy. Today Grant would install blinds in the living room, then begin the process of ripping out carpet.

As he entered the house, the aroma of apples and cinnamon greeted him. He had no doubt Maurie had been baking again. Perhaps she should open a café instead of a gift-basket store. "Hello?" he called. "Maurie? Taffy?"

No one responded, and the scent led him to the kitchen. It had been transformed over the past few days. Most of the moving clutter was gone, and Grant's handiwork had made things look new again. In the center of the kitchen table was some sort of baked-apple goodness. A note with his name on it rested next to the dish.

Grant,
Help yourself, be back in a couple of hours.
—Maurie

So he helped himself. He was getting spoiled in the mornings with delicious food. If he kept this up, he'd have to go up a pant size. After finishing off the strudel or tart or whatever it was, he brought in the long, narrow boxes of blinds that were in the bed of his truck. Then he proceeded to take down the ancient curtains and their rods. Dust plumed around him, making him sneeze more than once.

He took the dilapidated curtains and rods to his truck, so he could find a bigger Dumpster to deposit them. He hoped that Maurie didn't want to salvage them, because in his opinion, they were no loss.

By the time Grant had the blinds installed and had started on the carpet removal, Maurie and Taffy arrived at the house.

"Brought lunch," Taffy announced, holding up sacks from the Main Street Café. "Hope you're hungry." She breezed past him and headed into the kitchen.

"Sure," Grant said, and he looked over at Maurie, who'd come in behind Taffy.

Maurie's dark waves were pulled into a high ponytail, and she had blue paint smudges on her fitted T-shirt and yoga pants.

"Painting?" he asked.

She smiled, her green eyes scanning him. He noticed the appreciation, and that only made him hope Taffy would stay in the kitchen for a bit.

"Looks different in here," Maurie said, her gaze sliding to the window and the new blinds.

"Like it?" Grant asked, moving toward Maurie.

"I do." A small smile played on those pink lips of hers.

"Thanks for the apple—stuff—whatever it is."

Maurie smiled fully now. "Streusel."

"Whatever. It was delicious." He was close enough to touch her now, but *she* reached for *his* hand. That gesture alone sent a warm shiver through him.

"I'm glad to hear it." Slowly, she linked their fingers, and the slide of her warm skin against him created another shiver.

He really wished Taffy would go do a few errands on her own. He could hear her in the kitchen, opening drawers or something. Maybe he could give Maurie a brief kiss, one that would help with the burning building inside of him. He leaned down, and Maurie closed her eyes. Grant took that as a good sign.

He pressed his mouth against hers, softly, with only their

hands linking. Although he wanted to draw her closer, to feel more of her, to deepen their kiss, he kept the kiss brief.

When he lifted his head, Maurie kept her eyes closed for a few more seconds. He loved the way her long lashes lay against her cheek, just above a few of her freckles.

She opened her eyes, and the soft smile on her face made him want to kiss her again.

"Get it while it's warm," Taffy called from the kitchen.

Maurie bit her lip, gazing up at him as a faint blush stole across her cheeks. "So..."

"So... I guess you were painting?"

"Yeah," she said. "We made some good progress."

"You're okay to paint before you officially sign the closing docs?" Grant asked.

Maurie shrugged. "Jeff Finch gave us the green light."

Grant drew her just a little closer, because it was impossible to stop at one kiss with Maurie.

"I don't know about you guys," Taffy said, her voice suddenly in the room. She'd come out of the kitchen. "But soup is better hot, or at least warm."

Grant didn't move his gaze from Maurie. "Message received."

Taffy laughed, then turned on her heel and disappeared again.

Maurie sighed and placed her hand on Grant's chest. That wasn't going to help him keep her at arm's length.

"My roommate can be annoying," she said.

"I don't mind." He reluctantly stepped away. "But that soup does smell good. And my sister's ski clothes are in that bag over there."

Maurie turned to look at the bag. "Okay, I'll try on the stuff after we eat."

They walked into the kitchen, and Grant sat at the table with Taffy and Maurie.

He found it amusing how Taffy and Maurie teased each other, Taffy about how Maurie was so picky about her food, and Maurie accusing Taffy of eating only processed and chemically infused food.

"This is good," Maurie said about the squash soup they were eating. "I would have used toasted pine nuts and freshly grated parmesan as a garnish though."

"Only you would garnish soup," Taffy said with a smirk. "Soup's soup."

Maurie turned her green eyes on Grant. "What do you think?"

"About the soup?"

"About the garnish," Taffy said.

Grant looked from Taffy to Maurie. "Is there a right and wrong answer? Because I definitely want to give the right answer."

"Garnish or *no* garnish," Taffy said. "Simple as that."

He looked down at his soup. Squash wasn't his favorite, but it was decent. "Can't say I've ever considered the choice."

Taffy laughed. "See, Maurie. Two against one."

Maurie smirked. And then she grasped Grant's hand under the table and proceeded to eat with her left hand.

Grant was pretty sure Taffy knew what was going on.

This was nice, Grant decided. More than nice. He didn't know why now, of all months or all years, he was allowing himself to entertain thoughts of a future with more than just work, his son, and fighting with Joy. Maurie had been unexpected, and Grant was surprisingly fine with that.

Taffy finished her soup first and headed to her room, leaving them alone.

Maurie still held Grant's hand, and she turned to him. "What time do we need to leave for skiing?"

"About three-thirty," he said. "Does that still work?"

"Yeah," Maurie said.

The look in her eyes was so warm, so trusting, that Grant felt a twinge of guilt resurface. Would she look at him like that if she knew about his role that last night in Pine Valley? But he didn't have time to dwell on the thought for long, because Maurie leaned close and kissed him.

It was amazing how fast his pulse could thrum when they kissed. Before things could get any more intense, he drew away. He did have a job to do, and taking part of the afternoon off to go skiing would cut back on what he needed to finish today. "You're way too distracting, Maurie Ledbetter."

She smiled. "You're kind of irresistible, Grant Shelton."

His heart flipped.

The sound of a door opening—probably Taffy's—prevented Grant from following his instinct to kiss Maurie again.

"Back to work, I guess," he said, squeezing her hand, then rising from the table.

He felt Maurie's gaze on him as he left the kitchen, and he couldn't help the smile that seemed to be a permanent feature on his face.

Twelve

"I'm supposed to do what?" Maurie said, staring down at the long, narrow skis on her feet as she stood next to Grant at the bottom of the bunny hill.

Grant took hold of her arm. "Jab the boot of your toe into the clip, then step back, hard."

Maurie tried, but the ski boot was heavy and awkward, and the boot slipped off the ski. The ski slid away, marking a path along the snow-packed ground. Grant made a move to grab the ski.

"Here." He knelt next to her and grasped her calf to guide her boot into the clip. "Now put all your weight on your heel and push down."

Maurie did so, and miraculously the boot clipped into the ski. If it was this hard to get the skis on in the first place, what would the actual skiing be like? In another moment, she was clipped into both skis.

"Okay, here are your poles," Grant said. "Use them to balance while we get on the magic carpet."

"Magic carpet?"

Grant pointed to a moving thing that looked like a conveyor belt.

"Umm," Maurie hedged.

Grant only laughed. "I won't let you fall off. I don't think it's possible to fall off, but just in case, I'll be right behind you."

She watched kids who couldn't be more than four years old sidestep onto the conveyor thingy and ride up the bunny hill. If a little kid could do it, she could too, right? "All right." She gripped the ski poles probably a little too tightly.

Grant kept his hand on her elbow, and she walked-slash-glided toward the magic carpet.

"Keep your knees slightly bent," he said. "It's sort of like roller skating or ice skating."

Maurie kept her mouth shut because she hadn't done either. Had her childhood really been so void of the regular things that all kids seemed to do? Yes.

True to his word, Grant got her onto the magic carpet without her falling, and as the conveyor took them up the slope, Maurie watched other beginner skiers navigate the bunny hill. Some crashed. One kid was crying. But overall, the skiers were enjoying themselves. An older lady was skiing as slow as molasses. So apparently Maurie wouldn't be the only adult woman skiing for the first time.

"We're almost there," Grant said behind her. "Step off like you're getting off an escalator, but remember you have long skis attached to your feet, so try not to cross them."

"Okay," Maurie said in a faint voice as she gazed at the end of the magic carpet. She could do this. No one had fallen in front of her, and Grant was right behind her. She held her breath and stepped off, first her right foot, then her left. The ground was relatively flat, or so she thought. She started to slide backward, and she dug her poles into the ground, which only rooted her hands. Her skis were still moving.

Grant put his arm around her waist. "Easy there," he said in that deep voice of his.

Maurie would have enjoyed his closeness if it weren't for the fact she was on skis, with the potential of falling on her rear at any moment.

"Thanks," she said.

"Bend your knees more, and push against the snow as if you're the one in command," Grant said. "Let's get you turned around."

Maurie only wobbled a couple of times as she turned. She was pretty sure her thigh muscles were going to be plenty sore after this.

"Now," Grant said, "we're going to learn the pizza."

"What?" She must have sounded thoroughly confused, because Grant laughed.

"Put the tips of your skis together while keeping the backs spread apart." He moved away from her and demonstrated. "Like a pizza."

She watched him. How did he look so great in ski clothes? She looked like the Abominable Snowman in his sister's coat and ski pants. "So, a triangle?"

He grinned. "Exactly. But kids like the pizza version best. See those kids over there? They're doing the pizza."

Maurie followed his gaze. Sure enough. Two kids, probably five and eight, were moving down the hill, their skis in a triangle shape. They weren't going that fast, and they weren't falling either.

"Ready?" Grant asked.

Maurie took a deep breath. Supposedly this was fun, or it would become fun. She was ready. Moving forward with the aid of the ski poles, she focused on keeping her skis in a triangle shape. She went slow, and pretty much everyone passed her by, even a kid who was probably three years old at the most.

"You're doing great," Grant said, and Maurie wondered how painful this was for him.

But she only saw warmth in those blue eyes of his. By the time she reached the bottom of the bunny hill, she was going a little faster and was feeling more comfortable.

"You did great," Grant said. "Ready to go up again?"

"Sure." Maurie felt a bit breathless, but mostly from the fact that she'd actually skied down a mountain. Well, a bunny slope, but still.

By the third time down the bunny hill, Grant had taught her how to turn and how to stop.

And Maurie could admit that she was having fun. As long as Grant didn't try to talk her into getting onto a ski lift and coming down the higher slopes. Maybe she could forever ski the bunny hill.

Darkness had set in, and the slopes were lit by massive lights. Surprisingly, Maurie wasn't cold.

"Do you need a break?" Grant asked when they'd reached the bottom of the bunny hill for about the fifth time.

"No, I'm good," Maurie said.

"Okay, I think I need to teach you how to fall and how to get back up."

"There's a way to *fall*?" she asked.

"Yeah, so you, uh, don't break anything."

Maurie stared at him. "Like my bones or my skis?"

"Either," Grant said. "Come on. Let's get back on the magic carpet."

So she did, and Grant showed her how to let her body relax when she fell, and how to position her skis perpendicular to the slope in order to get them back on.

"I think this is the hardest part of skiing," Maurie said. "Getting these dang skis on."

Grant chuckled. "You'll get the hang of it. Just think of how far you've come in only a couple of hours."

It was true.

"Let's get drinks at the lodge," he said.

Maurie decided not to turn him down. She could only imagine how sore she'd be tomorrow. They left their skis on one of the racks, then walked into the lodge like a Big Foot couple. Clomping around in such giant boots felt awkward, but everyone else was wearing them too.

Grant unzipped his coat and hung it on a long rack by the door, where other coats hung. A ringing phone sounded, and Maurie said, "It's coming from your coat."

Grant unzipped the inside pocket and took out his phone. He sent the call to voicemail, then slipped it into his pants pocket.

Maurie peeled off her gloves and hung up her coat as well.

"Want to grab a table," Grant said, "and I'll get the drinks?"

There were only a couple of empty tables, so Maurie snagged one. She watched Grant order drinks and couldn't help but admire him. Her admiration was more than physical though; he was so different from Brandon and had been since she first knew Grant. Some people never changed, and that was a good thing for Grant.

When Grant reached the table with the drinks, his phone was ringing again.

"You can get that," Maurie said. "I don't mind."

"I probably should," he said. "Joy might be calling about Trent."

He answered his phone, and Maurie sipped at the hot chocolate. It was nice and steamy, although it could use a little more flavor. She tried not to listen in on Grant's conversation with his ex, but it was hard not to since he was sitting across from her.

"Of course I have no problem getting him, but will Trent be okay with that?" Grant said.

A few moments later he was off the phone, his brow furrowed.

"Is everything okay?"

Grant rubbed a hand down over his jaw. "Trent has strep throat, and tomorrow is Stone's company retreat. They were going to take him, since there's stuff for kids to do. But now he'll be miserable and probably still contagious if they take him."

"Poor kid," Maurie said.

"Yeah," Grant said. "And Joy wants him picked up tonight since she doesn't want to be dealing with taking care of him when she finishes packing in the morning."

Maurie nodded. "We should go then."

"I'm really sorry," he said, standing.

"No worries," Maurie said, standing as well. "Trent needs his dad right now."

"Well, I'm glad I get to see him, but not because he's sick," Grant said. "And I appreciate your understanding."

She smiled. "You're doing the right thing."

Grant paused by their coats. "Hey, do you want to ride with me to pick him up? It's about an hour drive each way."

Maurie was surprised by the offer, and she was even more surprised at her response. "Sure."

"Really?" His eyes were warm upon hers.

"Yeah, really." She didn't know why her heart was racing. Maybe it was because Grant had basically invited her to meet his *son*. Or maybe it was because she was curious about seeing Joy—of course, Maurie might not see her at all. She didn't know how Grant handled picking up his kid.

"Great." He handed over her coat.

He grasped her hand, and they left the lodge and headed

toward his SUV. He loaded his skis, then said, "I'll go check yours back in. See you in a minute."

"Okay," Maurie said before he shut the hatch of the SUV, and she was left to herself in the warming air. She estimated that she had at least ten minutes before Grant returned, so she called Taffy to give her an update.

"Wow, that's definitely the next step," Taffy said. "Are you sure you want to be this involved in his life?"

This was the most serious that Maurie had heard Taffy be toward Grant. "He asked, and I said yes. I was surprised myself."

Taffy laughed. "I'm *not* surprised." She lowered her voice. "If you're good with all of this, then I'm good. Know that I have your back."

"I know," Maurie said. "You always do. He's so different than Brandon, and I just feel . . . comfortable around Grant. Like we've known each other forever. Which we have in a way."

"I get it," Taffy said. "Remember, Pine Valley is a really small town, so, you know, if things go south . . ."

"True." Maurie saw Grant coming out of the lodge. "I've got to go." She hung up with Taffy and watched Grant approach. He looked worried, and Maurie wondered if he was thinking about Trent.

When he climbed in the truck, Maurie said, "Everything okay?"

Grant glanced over at her. "Fine," he said. "I have to gear myself up for seeing Joy. Usually I need a little more notice."

Thirteen

Grant hoped that this trip with Maurie to get his son wouldn't scare her off. But it was probably good for Joy to know that there was someone else in his life. No matter how new things with Maurie were. If he and Maurie continued dating, then Trent would be meeting her eventually. And now it would be sooner than later.

Besides, if Joy met Maurie, then she'd know who Trent was talking about when he returned home. Grant could very well imagine the tirade that Joy would bestow upon him if she learned about Maurie through Trent.

Yes, Grant knew things were moving pretty fast with Maurie, and he justified it with the fact that he'd known her years ago. He'd never connected with someone as quickly as Maurie, and he realized now that maybe their connection hadn't ever been lost. It had been there the whole time.

As they drove through the winter night, they talked mostly about Trent, but there were patches of silence as well. Comfortable silences. Something that Grant had never had with Joy. If she was quiet, it meant a storm was brewing.

By the time they pulled up to the gated community that housed Joy's home with Stone, nerves had settled in Grant's stomach. Although they'd been divorced almost four years, seeing Joy always brought back the hard memories of how controlling Joy was. How she'd treated him. How he'd allowed it.

Joy's house was lit up, lights spilling from the windows onto the winter lawn. Grant pulled into the driveway and looked over at Maurie. "You don't have to come in, but I'd like you to."

"I'll come in," Maurie said.

"Thanks," Grant said. "I'll probably be telling you that a lot tonight."

Maurie smiled. "You already have."

He climbed out of the SUV and opened Maurie's door, then they walked up to the front door, and Grant knocked. He rarely rang doorbells, since he always wondered if there could be a child sleeping inside a house. Old habit, he supposed.

The door opened seconds later, and Grant looked down to see his son. Trent's blue eyes and light-brown hair made the kid a mini-me of Grant. Just the sight of his son after so many weeks made Grant's heart swell.

Trent wrapped his arms about Grant's legs, and he stooped to hug his son and kiss the top of his head. "Hey, buddy," he said. "I heard you were sick."

"Yep," Trent said.

Grant crouched to meet him at eye level. "What happened?" At this close of inspection, Grant noticed how Trent's cheeks were pale, and his eyes had a drowsy look.

"It hurts to swallow." Trent pressed his fingers against his throat. "The doctor said I have a scratched throat."

"I can tell," Grant said. "Do you want to come stay with me for a few days?"

Trent nodded, his gaze solemn.

Grant smiled. "Good. My friend Maurie came with me to pick you up."

Trent looked up at Maurie and gave her a shy smile.

"Hi, Trent," Maurie said in a soft voice.

"I have a scratched throat," Trent said.

"Does it hurt?" Maurie asked.

Trent gave another solemn nod, then leaned against Grant. He picked up his son and straightened just as another voice rang out.

"Trent," Joy said. "I told you not to answer the door." She strode into the room, wearing a dark-green fitted dress and black stilettos, along with a generous amount of gold jewelry. Joy never did anything by half. She slowed when she saw Grant, and her gaze darted to Maurie. Joy's brows lifted, and in her pale-blue eyes, Grant could see all the questions she wanted to ask.

"Hi, Joy," he said. "This is Maurie."

Joy's eyes narrowed the slightest bit as she gave Maurie another once-over. Then she looked at Trent. "What did I tell you about answering the door, son?" Her tone of voice was both sweet and condescending.

"But it was Daddy," Trent said.

"It was your father *this time*, but we never know who might be at the door, remember?"

Trent's lower lip trembled. "I remember."

"Hey, buddy," Grant cut in. "Are you packed up?"

Trent kept his arms looped around Grant's neck and shrugged. "Mommy said she would pack because my throat is scratched."

"Strep," Joy corrected. "You have *strep*. And remember you can't share any germs."

"I remember," Trent repeated.

Grant spotted Trent's bag at the side of the entrance, and he bent to pick it up, still holding Trent. "Is this everything?" he asked Joy.

"Why don't you load him in the car, and then I can give you the instructions."

"Sure thing," Grant said.

Maurie walked out with them, and Joy still hadn't said a word to her. Grant got Trent situated in the SUV, and Maurie climbed into the passenger seat. When Grant shut Trent's door, he turned to see Joy standing right behind him.

And she didn't look happy.

Grant shoved his hands into his pockets.

"Who is that woman?" Joy hissed. "Our son is *sick*. Don't you think that should take priority over some . . . *woman*?"

Grant exhaled, his breath fogging in the cold night air. "Maurie was with me when you called. You know that Trent is always my priority, and that's why I'm here, and why you're going on a retreat, leaving him behind."

Joy's eyes widened, and Grant knew she was trying to figure out if he'd insulted her.

A headache had begun behind Grant's eyes. It had probably started the moment he'd talked to Joy on the phone earlier, but now it was stronger.

He reached for the driver's side door handle. "I'll text you updates."

"Wait." Joy sighed. "He needs the antibiotic twice a day. Keep it in the refrigerator. He'll be contagious until tomorrow morning, so don't share glasses with him." She looked past him as if she could see into the tinted windows in the dark. "Is that woman living with you?"

"No, and her name is Maurie, not *that woman*."

Joy puffed out a breath through her red-lined lips. "The bacteria of strep can keep living after twenty-four hours, so be sure to soak his toothbrush in hydrogen peroxide just in case. And only give him soft foods that won't hurt his throat. He can also have children's ibuprofen, but be sure to follow the dosage chart for his weight."

Grant nodded. "Got it. Anything else?"

Joy hesitated, and it was clear she had plenty more to say. But she pursed her lips and shook her head. Then she opened Trent's door. "Bye, sweetie. Daddy will take care of you, and I'll see you in a few days. Okay?"

Trent said something, but Grant didn't catch it. Joy shut the door, straightened, and stared at Grant for a moment. He waited for her next onslaught of words. But she turned and walked toward her house. When the front door shut, Grant released the breath he'd been holding. He climbed into the car.

Music was playing inside the car; Maurie must have turned on the radio. To drown out what Joy had said to him?

He glanced over at her, and she gave him a small smile.

Grant smiled back and reversed out of the driveway.

"You okay, buddy?" he asked Trent.

"Yeah," Trent said. "Maurie said she'd make me some pudding. Can I have some?"

Grant hid a chuckle. "Sure." He reached over and grasped Maurie's hand. She linked their fingers, and it was like a wave of peace washed over him.

"That wasn't so bad," Maurie said in a quiet voice a few minutes later.

Before answering, Grant glanced in the rearview mirror to see that Trent had fallen asleep. His heart tugged.

"The drive?" he whispered. "Or my ex-wife?"

"Both." Maurie squeezed his hand. "Joy seems pretty high maintenance, to say the least. But she loves her kid."

Grant couldn't deny it. He just wished she'd be a little less demanding about everything. "She is a good mom," he admitted. "Just a terrible ex-wife."

Maurie scoffed. "How are ex-wives supposed to be?"

"Yeah, you're right," he said. "I haven't heard anyone say how much they love and appreciate their exes."

"True."

The miles passed, and finally Grant said, "Do you ever hear from your dad?"

"No," Maurie said. "I don't even know if he's still alive, although I assume he is." She looked out the window. "My mom wouldn't ever talk about him, and eventually I stopped asking her questions. It kept the peace between us. Once I decided to stop hoping my dad would show up some day, it became a lot easier."

"It's hard to know the reasons a person acts the way they do," Grant said. "But he missed out."

She smiled. "Most definitely." She glanced at the sleeping Trent. "Poor kid. You don't need to worry about my house for the next few days."

"I'll play it by ear," Grant said. "If he perks up, then he can play with Julie's kids."

"Trent's a lucky kid despite all the heartache that Joy's caused you," Maurie said.

"I guess that's a good way to look at it," he said, pulling her hand up so that he could kiss the back of her hand. "Although I'm the one who feels lucky right now."

Maurie didn't say anything for a moment. "I wasn't expecting to see you when I returned to Pine Valley. So this is all kind of surreal for me."

"Tell me about it." Grant glanced over at her, and their gazes briefly connected. His heart rate increased. Because he knew that he could very well fall in love with this woman. And because he knew he needed to tell her about his role all those years ago.

When they arrived at his place, Grant's thoughts raced as

he wondered what his apartment looked like. He wasn't in the habit of having company over—at least not female company—but at least it was clean due to the fact that he was hardly ever home.

Grant parked and looked at Trent.

"Still asleep," Maurie whispered.

"I'll carry him, if you can get the doors." He handed her the keys, then he climbed out of the SUV and scooped Trent into his arms. Trent barely stirred and turned his face against Grant's neck.

Maurie grabbed Trent's duffle bag, then walked with Grant toward the apartment building. He told her which apartment was his so that she could unlock the door. She opened the door and turned on a single light, which was enough to guide him to Trent's bedroom.

Maurie turned down the *Incredibles* bedding, then she slid off Trent's slippers before Grant pulled the covers over him.

They left the bedroom quietly, and Grant positioned the door ajar.

Maurie handed over the duffle bag, and Grant carried it into the kitchen. He flipped on lights and set the bag on the table. Inside, he found the antibiotic to be refrigerated, and a bottle of children's ibuprofen.

Maurie leaned against the kitchen counter, watching him. "Do you own or rent this place?"

"Rent," Grant said, shutting the fridge door. He gazed about the kitchen, seeing it as she must see it. Cheap countertops, scuffed kitchen table, plain gray linoleum, cupboards that could use some sanding and new stain. "I know what you're thinking."

Maurie tilted her head, and a smile crept into her green eyes. "You do?"

"I do." He walked toward her, and she watched him approach, unmoving.

"So you can read my mind now?" she teased.

He stopped close to her, not touching her yet. "I don't think I'd ever be able to read a woman's mind, but I might come close."

Maurie laughed. "Then what am I thinking right now?"

"You're wondering why I live in such a cheap apartment when I'm a carpenter by trade," he said.

"It's probably the philosophy of someone who cleans houses all day for a living, and the last thing she wants to do is clean her own house when she gets home at night."

"That's a good analogy," Grant said, resting his hands on her hips.

Maurie put her hands on his biceps. "But that wasn't what I was thinking."

"Should I keep guessing?" Grant asked, leaning closer. "Or will you tell me?"

Maurie slid her hands up his arms and over his shoulders. "I was thinking you should come over here and kiss me."

"You're not scared off by my ex-wife and kid?"

She moved her hands behind his neck and tugged him closer. "I think you're an amazing man, Grant Shelton."

He smiled. Then he did kiss her.

Fourteen

Maurie opened her eyes, and the first thing she realized was that she wasn't in her bed in her small house. She was . . . *Oh no.*

She sat up, blinking against the dimness of the room. And then she remembered. She and Grant had been watching a movie . . . She looked around the living room to see that the television was off. Someone had covered her with a blanket. Her cell phone was on the coffee table, and she picked it up. 6:00 a.m.

She must have fallen asleep during the movie, and Grant hadn't woken her up, but let her sleep on the couch.

There was a text from Taffy sent about midnight. *Won't wait up for you. Hope you're having fun. Wink. Wink.*

Maurie should probably text her back, but Taffy knew she was with Grant and *his sick kid*, for heaven's sake. Despite herself, Maurie smiled. Then she yawned. The house was completely silent. Was Grant still asleep—in his bedroom, she assumed? Was Trent still sleeping? Had he awakened feeling sick, and she slept right through everything?

She didn't have her car so unless she called Taffy, she was stuck here until Grant woke up. Moving off the couch, she stretched her sore neck. She wondered what time she'd fallen asleep, and how Grant had managed to move without waking her up.

She found the bathroom, then went into the kitchen to get a drink of water. An inspection of the fridge revealed why Grant loved her baking so much. He had a few basics, but that was it. Nothing much in the pantry either, so baking was out of the question.

With Trent's sore throat, he'd want something soft anyway, so she elected to make scrambled eggs. She hoped the kid liked eggs. Trying to keep as quiet as possible, she found a frying pan that looked barely used, then whisked the eggs together and grated a block of cheese. She almost laughed aloud when she found salt and pepper packets. Grant didn't even have his own shakers. The man needed a trip to Walmart.

She didn't expect to find placemats, which she didn't, but was surprised he had a healthy stack of napkins in one of the cupboards.

The eggs were simmering nicely when a voice spoke from the hallway. "Are you making pudding?"

Maurie turned to see Trent. His face was flushed from sleep, and one side of his brown hair stuck up. His blue eyes were so much like Grant's that Maurie agreed there was no way Trent was someone other than Grant's son.

"I'm making scrambled eggs," Maurie said. "Do you like them?"

Trent gave a solemn nod.

"Well then, come on and have a seat." She patted the back of one of the chairs.

He gave her the smallest smile, then climbed on the chair. He stayed kneeling so that his belly was even with the top of the table.

"Daddy's still sleeping," Trent said, his blue eyes following every movement of Maurie's.

"Did you check on him?" she asked.

"Yeah, he's sleeping in my bed." Trent laughed. "It's funny. I told him he was too big, but he said that he wanted to be with me."

Maurie nodded. Grant sharing a twin-sized bed with his son was funny, but endearing too.

"Because I'm sick."

"You are sick," Maurie said, holding back a smile. "Does your throat still hurt?"

He pressed his fingers to his throat and visibly swallowed. Maurie didn't miss the wince.

"It's scratched," he said.

She didn't correct him like his mother had. "Do you want a drink?" Maurie asked, moving to fetch a glass.

Trent took the glass and drank at least half of it. "I was thirsty."

Maurie couldn't help but laugh. She wasn't around kids a lot, and never one on one. It was adorable how he blurted things out.

"Are you going to make pudding after this?" Trent asked, poking his finger in his water.

Should she tell him to stop? "Your dad doesn't have all the ingredients for pudding, so I have to go back to my place and make it."

Now Trent had his entire fist in the water glass.

"Careful, it might spill," Maurie said.

Trent sighed. "That's what my mom says."

Maurie bit her lip to keep from laughing. Trent proceeded to take his hand out of the water, then he wiped his wet hand on the front of his long-sleeved T-shirt he'd been wearing when they'd picked him up last night.

Maurie scooped the scrambled eggs into three bowls. More for the bowl she'd give to Grant. There wasn't any bread to make toast, so this would be a single-course meal. "Do you want salt and pepper?" Maurie asked as she ripped open one of the packets.

"Mommy says Stone can't have salt," Trent said.

Maurie nodded. "What about you? Can you have salt?"

Trent shrugged his small shoulders. "I dunno."

"How about I put a little bit on," Maurie said. "Then once you eat, you can have your medicine."

"For my scratched throat?" Trent pushed on his throat again.

"Yep." Maurie set the bowls on the table, along with the spoons. Then she sat by Trent.

"Look at the smoke," Trent said, pointing at the steam.

Maurie smiled. "The eggs are hot. Do you want to blow on them?"

"Okay," Trent said in a cheerful tone. And he did just that.

"I think you can take a bite now," Maurie said after he continued blowing.

They finished their eggs, and Maurie was glad that Trent seemed to like them. "Hey," she said in a quiet voice. "I'll go see if your dad's still asleep. Be right back, okay?"

"Okay," Trent said in a glum voice, which gave Maurie pause.

"Do you want to help me?" she asked.

His face immediately brightened.

"We have to be really quiet though," she said.

"Like mouses? I can walk like mouses."

"Yes, like mice." Maurie smiled as Trent climbed off the chair, then walked on his toes down the hall. The sun had risen, so there was enough light coming in through the living room, and she didn't have to turn on the hall light. She followed Trent, knowing that at any minute, they might make enough noise to alert Grant.

But when she pushed the bedroom door open, Grant was spread out on the twin bed, sound asleep. He was on his back, one arm behind his head, and . . . he wasn't wearing a shirt.

Maurie didn't move for a moment. Who in the world didn't sleep with a shirt on in the middle of winter? Apparently Grant Shelton didn't. At least he was wearing running shorts and not just boxers or something.

And watching him sleep without the aforementioned shirt made her cheeks heat. She already knew his shoulders were broad and that he was in good shape from manual labor. But she found herself scanning the length of his torso and his perfectly carved muscles. She instinctively knew that his chest and stomach would be solid, yet warm and soft to the touch.

Maurie swallowed. She should really stop ogling him, back out, and shut the door. Instead, she watched the steady rise and fall of Grant's chest as he breathed. Only the worry of Trent waking his sleeping dad brought Maurie back to her senses sooner than later.

"He's still sleeping," Trent said in a rather loud whisper.

"We should go out," Maurie whispered back, holding out her hand.

Trent took it, and they stepped into the hall.

Maurie pulled the door almost closed without letting it click shut.

Trent's hand was warm and a little sweaty. When they reached the kitchen, Maurie bent to feel his forehead.

"Are you hot?" she asked.

Trent shrugged. "I dunno."

"Well, since your daddy's sleeping, I'll give you your medicine." Maurie wished she'd had more experience with little kids, but how hard could it be to give medicine to a kid? She pulled the medicine of pink liquid out of the fridge. The instructions were on the bottle, of course, and Grant had left the dropper on the counter.

Maurie measured out the medicine. "Okay, ready?"

Trent opened his mouth and closed his eyes.

Well, that was easy. Maurie squirted the medicine in his mouth. "Swallow."

He did.

"Good job," she said. "We'll be sure to tell your dad that you had your first dose."

She eyed the ibuprofen on the counter. "Does your mom give you two medicines at once?"

Trent nodded. "The purple one too. Mommy says it's for my femur."

It took Maurie a second to decipher. "Your fever?"

"That's what I said."

Maurie pulled out her phone from her pocket and googled: *can you take ibuprofen with amoxicillin.* Apparently you could unless you were into all-natural healing. She picked up the bottle and read the dosage chart. "You're four?" she asked Trent.

"Almost five."

"Okay," Maurie said. "How much do you weigh?"

"Fifty-hundred."

Maurie blinked. "Um. Let's go see if your dad has a scale in the bathroom."

So Trent went with her to the bathroom, and thankfully there was a scale on the floor. "Forty-six pounds," Maurie said. "You're growing up."

She measured out the right amount of the liquid ibuprofen, then Trent swallowed that down too.

Now what?

"Do you want to read or play games?"

Trent yawned. "I'm tired."

Maurie ruffled his hair. She wasn't sure where that gesture of affection had come from. "I'm sure you are. Maybe we can find something to watch on TV?"

"I can only watch kid shows," Trent pronounced.

Maurie smiled. "Kid shows it is. Come on."

Trent put his hand in hers, which made her heart soar for some reason.

They walked into the living room, and Maurie settled Trent onto the couch with the blanket she'd had earlier. She turned on the TV at low volume and clicked through channels until Trent told her to stop at a SpongeBob cartoon.

Not her favorite, but Maurie didn't want to abandon Trent on the couch. So she sat by him, and almost instantly, he snuggled against her. Maurie's heart melted a little more. This kid was adorable, and she wasn't even related to him. She wrapped her arm around him and became caught up in the current adventure of SpongeBob.

She started to feel tired and closed her eyes for a moment. She wasn't sure what had woken her up, but when she next opened her eyes, Trent had fallen asleep. Something in the kitchen clinked, and she looked over to see Grant leaning against the counter, eating the bowl of scrambled eggs.

He smiled when their gazes connected.

And . . . he was still shirtless. Maurie's face went hot.

"Good morning," he said in that rumbling voice of his.

"Good morning." She looked down at Trent. "He ate, and I gave him his medicine. I guess he was still tired."

"Thanks for making eggs," Grant said. "I was starving."

Maurie's face was still hot. Because she couldn't quite look away from his bare torso. He put the bowl in the sink, then he filled a glass with water from the tap. She watched as he drank down the entire glass. She was still watching when he turned to catch her staring at him.

She was totally blushing. Surely he noticed.

And now he was walking toward her.

Maurie could only watch him because she was pretty much stuck in one position with a kid sleeping on her.

"Do you want me to move him?" Grant asked in a soft voice, looking from her to Trent.

"No, he's okay." She swallowed as Grant sat next to her on the couch. He smelled warm and musky. "Besides, I want to see if Mr. Krabs makes it to the party."

Grant chuckled softly. "I think I remember this episode."

"Don't give away the ending."

Grant linked their hands together, his fingers warm against hers. "I wouldn't dare."

Maurie exhaled as she tried to tamp down the heat rushing through her. Sitting on the couch in the early morning, with Grant on one side of her and his sleeping son nestled against her on the other side, created emotions she couldn't identify. She'd had a boyfriend before, but she'd never felt so . . . safe? At home?

Her home life had never been like this. Quiet, simple, warm.

Was this what it was like? Being surrounded by goodness and caring? Maybe even love?

Her eyes stung, and she blinked back any threatening tears. She really should focus on Mr. Krabs's mission.

"Thanks for all this," Grant said, his thumb caressing the back of her hand. "I didn't mean for you to be an early-morning babysitter."

Maurie smiled, although her heart and pulse were doing crazy things. She felt like laughing and crying at the same time. "Well, I didn't mean to fall asleep on your couch. So thanks for the blanket."

Grant smiled and then he was leaning toward her.

She let her eyes drift shut just before Grant kissed her. It was tender, soft, and warm. And oh, so sweet. He drew away but lingered, and she knew if Trent wasn't in the same room, she would probably explore just what his chest felt like.

When Grant kissed her a second time, equally soft, she was the one who drew back first. "Um, can you put on a shirt?"

His blue eyes crinkled at the corners. "Is there a problem?"

"Yes, you without a shirt."

He grinned, then rose to his feet. "I should probably take a shower too. Are you okay for a few minutes with Trent?"

"Of course," she said. "Now, shoo."

Fifteen

Grant answered Joy's call on the first ring, trying not to sound full of dread, even though he was. He'd dropped off Trent thirty minutes before, and Joy wasn't home. So Grant had relinquished him to Stone. The two men had a conciliatory relationship, and that was just fine with Grant.

But Grant also knew that Joy would get an earful of stories about Maurie.

She'd been with him and Trent a lot over the past three days. Maurie had made Trent pudding and all kinds of treats—all of which he had loved as he started feeling better. Taffy had even jumped in and spoiled the kid, buying him a set of Hot Wheels that Trent kept in his pockets at all times.

The four of them had gone to the latest Pixar movie in the theaters. And Grant and Maurie had taken Trent to the ice-skating rink, where Grant learned that Maurie had never been ice skating.

"Hi, Joy," Grant said, picking up his phone.

"How much sugar did Trent have?" Joy said without any other type of greeting.

"Today, or over the past three days?"

There was a pause, and Trent pictured the way her bright, lipsticked mouth would purse before she came up with a controlled answer.

"He says he has a tummy ache," Joy said, in that so-familiar accusatory tone of hers.

Okay, so that was a game-changer. "He didn't have any candy today," Grant said in a more subdued tone. "Scrambled eggs for breakfast, chicken strips and apple slices for lunch. He ate fruit snacks on the way to your house." Since that first morning Maurie had made scrambled eggs, Trent had asked for them the next two mornings.

Joy exhaled audibly. "Okay, well maybe it's the antibiotic. One of my friends said that after a few days, an antibiotic can make your stomach upset."

"Well, keep me posted if it gets worse," Grant said. Trent hadn't complained to him, but he hated to think his son might start feeling sick again.

"And you told me you weren't living with that woman," Joy said.

It took Grant a second to catch up with her change of subject. "Maurie? She has a name, you know. And she doesn't live with me."

"Trent said she makes the best scrambled eggs," Joy said.

First of all, maybe the scrambled eggs were for dinner, and second of all, Grant owed Joy no explanation about the woman he was dating. "Trent's right. They're excellent."

Joy puffed out a breath. "You know that all of your decisions affect Trent's life."

"Yes, as do *yours*," Grant said in a pointed voice. Where was his vote when Joy decided to move miles away and move in with her boyfriend, Stone? They weren't even married, yet Grant was expected to play along with everything they decided for Trent.

"It's hard to leave my son, Grant," Joy said. "I don't want to have to worry about what he's experiencing when he's not in my home."

Now Grant was angry. "He's my son too, Joy. And you know that I'll do anything for Trent, *except* stay out of his life. I can email over the custody agreement if you've somehow misplaced it."

Joy said nothing for a moment, and then she hung up.

Grant wasn't surprised. She hung up on him regularly. He just hated to think of all the fun and love that Trent experienced when he was with him, and then Trent had to return to his mother.

Grant stayed lost in his turbulent thoughts until he pulled up to Maurie's house. She was officially closing on the store this week and would be holding the grand opening the following week. He turned off the ignition of his SUV and gazed at the front of the house for a moment. Memories of the past now collided with more recent memories.

Seeing her with Trent these past few days had done something to Grant's heart that he hadn't expected. There had been a time when he'd had no interest in dating, no interest in getting into another relationship, because he'd determined that his life was full enough with work and Trent. But the past few days had shown him that there was room for more. And that *more* was better.

Trent had been absolutely taken with Maurie.

Grant was too.

Which meant he had to tell Maurie about their past. He'd ask her to dinner tonight, so they could be assured to be separated from Taffy.

He climbed out of his SUV and strode up to the house. His equipment was inside; all he had left was some electrical work to replace the light fixtures.

Maurie had told him to walk in, so he did, and immediately the scent of baked goods struck him. He made his way to the kitchen, where he could hear some noise. Maurie was standing at the stove, stirring something in a pan.

Her green eyes met his, and she smiled.

Grant's heart flipped over. He wished that tonight was already over with and everything was good and normal between them.

"Hi," she said. She was wearing black jeans and a faded pink sweater that hugged her curves. Her hair was pulled into a twist, exposing the elegance of her neck. "Want to try some wassail? It's a new recipe."

Grant didn't see Taffy anywhere, so he took the wooden spoon from Maurie and set it on the counter, then he drew Maurie into his arms.

Maurie laughed as her arms went about his neck. "Is that a *yes* or *no*?"

"It's a *maybe in a minute*." Grant kissed her, long and slow, because he was being selfish. Because he knew things could very well change between them. And because he didn't want to forget these moments with Maurie.

She pressed against him and kissed him back. Grant pulled her closer, running his hands up her back, then tangling them into her hair. He couldn't get enough of her, which meant he had to stop.

He reluctantly drew away.

"How was Trent on the drive?" she asked, her fingers brushing against the nape of his neck.

"Chattered like he was a sports announcer."

Maurie laughed. "I guess he's better, then?"

"Yeah, except Joy called and said he had a stomachache."

A crease formed between Maurie's brows, and Grant wanted to smooth it away. "I'm pretty sure he's okay, though," he said.

"I hope so," Maurie said. "I already miss him."

Grant nodded. "Me too." He both loved and hated that Maurie was attached to Trent. It would make his confession all that harder.

His heart was pounding, and it wasn't because he held a beautiful and inviting woman in his arms. It was because he knew he had to tell her before any more time passed.

"Uh, Maurie, I've been meaning to talk to you about something," he said in a slow voice.

She tilted her head. "Okay."

When he didn't say anything right away, her eyes grew wary.

"Let's talk outside," he said, glancing toward the hallway. He didn't want Taffy interrupting. He grasped Maurie's hand, and they left the house.

Once inside the SUV, he started the engine and turned up the heater.

"What's going on, Grant?" she asked, folding her arms and lifting her brows.

Why did her eyes have to be so beautiful and her lips so inviting?

He exhaled. "First, I need to apologize. There's something I should have told you when I came to your house to do the bid. The timing didn't seem right, and I . . ." He paused and lifted a hand to brush away a lock of hair that had fallen against her cheek.

Maurie merely stared at him, confusion on her face.

"I had wondered about you for years."

A slight smile touched her face.

"I was worried, actually," he said, looking away for a moment.

"You're a sweet man, Grant Shelton," she said.

He grasped her hand, and Maurie easily linked her fingers with his.

"Don't say that," he insisted in a quiet voice. "I . . . On your last night in Pine Valley, I came to your house. I was going to invite you to the high school dance."

Her lips parted with surprise.

"I wasn't going to do anything fancy," he said. "Just knock on your door and talk to you." She smiled, but Grant couldn't make himself join her.

"It was probably about nine thirty at night," he continued, "and I knew it was late for a school night, but the lights were on at your house."

Her smile faded, and Grant's heart rate sped up.

"My mom's party," she whispered.

"Yeah," Grant said. "The music was loud, and there were a few cars in front of your house. I figured they were your mom's friends. So I waited a while, trying to build up my courage. I didn't really want to face a bunch of people when I tried to talk to you."

Maurie nodded and bit her lip.

"But then . . ." Grant looked down at their clasped hands. Her skin was so smooth, and seeing her hand in his made him feel protective. "As I started up the walkway, the front door burst open, and a man came stumbling out. Your mom was right behind him. It was Joe. And your mom was yelling at him for cheating on her. She threw a beer bottle at him."

Maurie's face had gone still.

Grant had to continue, get it all out. "Joe ducked, but then he turned around and charged after her, cursing. I think I was in shock, and I didn't really know what to do. I could only think of you inside that house and being hurt by that man, or Joe turning on your mom."

Maurie turned her head to look out the front window.

"So I called the cops," Grant said quietly. "By the time they came, everyone else had gone home. It was just you and your mom inside. Still, I stayed on the other side of the street, afraid to identify myself. While the cops were inside your house, I went back home."

Maurie pulled her hand away and wiped at her cheeks.

His eyes burned with his own tears, and he wished she'd look at him. Say something. Anything. "Maurie, you have to know that I had no idea you'd be taken from your home and put in foster care. And I didn't intend for your mom to get arrested." He blew out a breath and rubbed his face. "If I could go back, I wouldn't have called. I feel like because of me, your whole life was turned upside down."

Maurie didn't move, didn't speak. Tears dripped down her face, and Grant wanted to pull her into his arms. Soak up her tears. But he felt a divide forming between them.

He knew the only thing he could do now was wait for her answer.

"My mother's problems weren't your fault," she said at last.

Relief should have flooded through Grant, but he was still on edge. "I know, but I'm sorry. I made a decision that I can't ever take back."

Maurie gave a small nod. "And my life was already upside down." Her voice trembled as she looked at her twisting hands. "I knew that someone must have called the cops, and I never really thought of who it might have been. Things happened in a whirlwind, and I probably still haven't fully processed that night."

"I wish I could go back and change things," Grant said. "I wish I had just knocked on your door instead of—"

Maurie held up her hand. "My mom did belong in jail, at least according to the law." She wiped at her cheeks again. "I need some time to digest this all."

"I understand," Grant said, his heart heavy. He wanted to

take her hand again, to pull her into his arms, to have her accept his comfort. His love. Because he knew he was in love with her, and this was perhaps the very worst time to realize it.

Maurie exhaled a shaky breath. She glanced at him, then looked away, and Grant hated the misery that was in her eyes.

"I think I need to be by myself for a while." She popped open the door before he could respond.

Grant watched her walk back into the house. He'd never felt so helpless before. Not even when Joy said she was going to fight for full custody of Trent just because she knew it would hurt him. At least then Grant knew he could hire a lawyer to represent him.

Had he let things go too far with Maurie? Had she just walked away from him for good? Was it over before things had really started?

Grant wrapped his hands around the steering wheel, squeezing until his knuckles went white. What he wouldn't give to go back to that fateful night. He could have knocked on her door. Stood up to Joe. Talked to Maurie. Or even left and returned the next day to talk to her.

Grant closed his eyes and exhaled. There was literally nothing he could do to change the past. And it had been the right thing to tell Maurie. Now he'd have to live with the fallout. He opened his eyes and stared at Maurie's house, feeling as if he'd just shed a warm coat and was standing in the middle of an icy blizzard.

Sixteen

Maurie went through the motions over the next few days, checking off things on her long to-do list. The grand opening of Every Occasion was on Friday, which happened to be the day before Valentine's Day.

Maurie's emotions were all over the place though. Taffy knew something was up, but Maurie had simply said she wasn't ready to talk about it, and thankfully Taffy had respected that. The store was coming together nicely, and seeing the progress each day sent warm bursts through Maurie's heart.

But then she'd return home in the evenings, see new evidence of Grant's progress, and almost collapse beneath the weight of memories. And grief. Intellectually she knew that Grant had done the right thing—it could have very well been someone else who'd called the cops that night. Did it really matter that it was Grant?

No, she told herself over and over.

But she couldn't quite get over the emotional side of it.

Grant had come to ask her to a dance. He'd seen the

awfulness that was her life—a life she'd hoped to hide from regular people. And Grant had taken action . . . had called in the law in order to correct the situation. If Maurie had found that out as a teenager, she would have been mortified knowing that the boy she had a crush on had been a witness.

But the other, more dangerous thoughts kept circulating inside her mind. What if Grant hadn't called the cops? Her mom wouldn't have been arrested. Maybe she would have cleaned up her act. Gotten into rehab like she'd talked about more than once. Maybe her mother would still be *alive*.

The thought haunted Maurie.

Certainly, Grant wasn't responsible for her mother's poor choices, but . . .

Maurie pulled up to the curb of the house.

"Penny for your thoughts," Taffy said from the passenger seat.

Maurie looked over at her best friend; she'd almost forgotten she was there. "Sorry, I'm not trying to ignore you."

Taffy rested a hand on her arm. "You can tell me anything, Maurie. When you're ready, of course."

Maurie nodded, tears stinging her eyes. "I know. And thank you. It's just hard because . . ." She couldn't finish.

"Can you tell me what he did?" Taffy said in a soft voice. "Do I need to break some kneecaps?"

Maurie gave a half laugh. "No, it wasn't . . . recent." She took a deep breath and told Taffy what Grant's role had been the night she'd been taken into foster care. Apparently all deep confessions happened in idling cars. When she finished, Taffy didn't say anything for a moment.

Maurie fully expected her friend to go through the same litany that had been in her own head.

Instead, Taffy turned to look at Maurie. "You need to make peace with your mom."

Maurie blinked. "What? She's dead."

Taffy nodded. "You can still make peace. I don't know what it will look like. Maybe a conversation at her gravesite?"

Shaking her head, Maurie clenched her hands into fists. "I can't go there."

"What do you think will happen if you go?"

Maurie hesitated, then said, "That I'll spiral into that dark place again. That the memories of my mom will be too hard to deal with?"

"I could come with you," Taffy said.

She'd offered more than once, and Maurie had always turned her down. On one hand, Maurie knew Taffy was right—there would probably be some closure if she went to her mom's gravesite. On the other hand, Maurie had tried to close the door on her past, and she didn't want to reopen it. Grant's confession had cracked the door open far enough.

"Whatever you decide," Taffy said, "I'm still going to be here for you. But I'd hate to see you throw away a very good part of your future for something in the past that can't be changed."

The tears were back. "You think Grant is my future?" Maurie whispered.

"He's crazy about you," Taffy said.

Maurie wiped at her cheeks. "I think I'm in love with him."

Taffy laughed softly. "Of course you are."

"Why does it hurt so much then?"

"Oh, hon." Taffy hugged her.

Maurie closed her eyes and squeezed Taffy back as if she could somehow squeeze away the pain of forgiving her mom, and even forgiving Grant. Her therapist had long ago told Maurie to forgive herself, and to stop second-guessing every conversation and choice made around her mother. Her mother had been the adult, Maurie the child.

Still . . . Maurie found her mind going back to that place again of deep regret.

When Taffy drew away, Maurie felt calmer. Maybe she *could* visit her mother's gravesite. And maybe she'd take Taffy along.

"Feeling better?" Taffy asked, her eyes full of compassion.

Maurie sniffled. "I'm going to bake an apple pie."

Taffy laughed. "Of course you are, and I'm going to eat it. And I'm sure Grant will be eating leftovers when he shows up in the morning."

At the mention of Grant, Maurie felt another twinge in her heart. She missed him. So much. She wanted to know how Trent was doing. She missed that kid too. Maurie sighed and opened the car door. "Apple pie it is."

Taffy followed her into the house, and while Maurie prepared the crust, Taffy brought her laptop into the kitchen. While Taffy responded to customers and confirmed orders, Maurie mixed and rolled the crust, then set it to chill in the fridge while she cored and peeled apples. Baking brought a sense of calm over her, and as she worked, she could think more clearly. The emotions that had so wracked her body seemed to fade, and in their place, she thought about her mother's gravesite.

She could go there in the morning, with Taffy. Maybe even take some flowers. Tell her mom about the new shop on Main Street. Then . . . maybe she could talk to Grant. Apologize to him at the very least. After these past days of silence, she was sure that Grant was probably fed up with the drama. He'd been through enough with his ex-wife.

Maurie ignored the tears welling in her eyes and stirred the sliced apples into a mixture of cinnamon, sugar, and nutmeg. By the time she'd finished the lattice strips of the upper pie crust, she'd determined that tomorrow morning would be the time to visit her mom's gravesite. And she wouldn't change her mind.

"Taffy," Maurie said.

Taffy looked up from her laptop. "Hmm?"

"Will you come with me to the Pine Valley Cemetery tomorrow morning?" Maurie said. "Early, before Grant shows up to work."

"Of course, hon," Taffy said. "I'll be ready."

More questions showed in Taffy's expression, but she didn't press for any other information, and for that, Maurie was grateful.

When the pie was safely in the oven, Maurie walked about the house, looking for the new changes that Grant had finished that day. All the light fixtures had been upgraded and were in working order. He'd installed a new vanity in the bathroom, so now it matched the tile above the bathtub.

She walked into her bedroom, where he'd installed blinds and redone the baseboards. He'd set the soft-blue paint she'd picked out on a tarp in the corner of the bedroom. Grant had already spackled all the cracks and holes in the walls. He'd also taped the new baseboards with blue painter's tape. She'd told him she'd do the painting after the grand opening of her store, and then they could order carpet from his carpet-layer friend.

Now Maurie didn't know if that was going to happen. She hadn't even spoken to Grant since the day of his confession.

She settled onto her bed and pulled one of the pillows to her chest. She'd spent most of her childhood in this bedroom, and although it looked different with the new bed and bedding, and the filled-in cracks on the wall, she could still visualize every crack and hole. Shapes she'd stared at until it became too dark at night. She used to watch the evening sunlight advancing across her room until the gold-orange was replaced by violet. She'd read under the covers with a flashlight and kept her door locked when her mom had her "friends" over.

Although the house was quiet now, the echoes of music and laughter from her mom's parties still seemed to seep through the walls. Maurie climbed off her bed and knelt on the floor, in front of the paint cans. She used the metal opener to pop open the lid of the first can. For some reason she'd always loved the smell of paint.

Next she picked up the wooden stick and plunged it into the thick paint. She watched the paint swirl as she stirred, then she drew out the stick. Before she realized what she was doing, she'd pulled her hair into a ponytail and picked up one of the brushes.

She dabbed it onto the wall right over a spackled crack that she always thought looked like the letter *J*. She stood back and surveyed the color. With the paint, the crack was no longer noticeable. She painted over another spackled crack, then another, until the entire wall looked like an abstract blue-and-white painting. She poured some paint into a roller pan, then used one of the new rollers. The paint went on quickly and smoothly with the roller, and soon she had an entire wall finished.

Switching again to the brush, she finished off the corners.

"What are you doing?" Taffy's voice came from the doorway of the bedroom.

Maurie turned. "Painting."

Taffy placed her hands on her hips. "I can see that . . . I thought we were going to paint after the store opened."

Maurie filled up the roller with more blue paint. "Plans changed."

"Do you want my help?"

"I think I'm good," Maurie said. "Just working out some things."

Taffy nodded, and when she left the room, Maurie moved the bed and single bedside table. She hadn't purchased a dresser yet, so she piled the clothes from the closet on top of the bed. She wouldn't be able to sleep in the bedroom with the paint fumes anyway.

Maurie finished sometime around one in the morning with a second coat, and then she crashed on the couch.

Her alarm went off at 6:30 a.m., and at first she was disoriented as to why she was on the couch. Then she remembered. She dragged herself to her feet and walked to her bedroom to survey what she'd done the night before. After flipping on the light, she walked in. The walls were beautiful. Unflawed, unmarred, and uncracked.

She pressed a finger to several spots on the wall. The paint was mostly dry and didn't need a third coat.

Maurie jumped in the shower, and by the time she was ready to go, Taffy was making awful instant coffee in the kitchen.

"Let's stop at the Main Street Café," Maurie said. "Anything is better than that."

"In a hurry to get out of here before You-Know-Who shows up?"

Instinctively, Maurie glanced at the digital clock on the microwave. It was almost 7:30, and Grant came around 8:00 a.m. She shrugged. "I'll be in the car, and I'm stopping at the café, so whatever you choose to drink here is your choice."

"I see you left out the pie with a note," Taffy said, a smile in her voice.

Maurie had written a note to Grant before crashing on the couch. He could have the whole pie if he wanted. "I did."

Taffy eyed her. "I'm ready if you are."

"I'm ready."

Seventeen

Grant fully expected Maurie's car to be gone by the time he arrived at her house, since it had been the past several mornings. So why did he feel that stab of disappointment when he pulled up to the curb?

She and Taffy were putting in all kinds of hours working at the store, and Grant suspected that Maurie was carefully avoiding him. Well, after today, she wouldn't have to worry about him anymore.

He'd finish the last couple of things, then clear his stuff out. He'd leave the carpet layer's card on the table, along with his own thank-you note. And that would be that.

Grant opened the front door to Maurie's house. As usual, she'd left it unlocked.

And, as usual, the house smelled heavenly, like something baking. And . . . new paint.

Grant ventured into the kitchen and saw the apple pie in the middle of a cleaned-off table.

Maurie had left a note. Nothing personal, just telling him to help himself. Grant wasn't hungry though, and no matter how delicious the pie smelled or looked, he decided he'd leave it for the women.

He followed the smell of paint and walked into Maurie's room. Which was now completely blue. It appeared she and Taffy had worked half the night too. Grant smiled. The blue looked great, and the room seemed totally different. He hoped that Maurie was happy with it.

He walked out of the bedroom and set to work. The other day he'd told Taffy that he was willing to help move any final things into the store, but she'd said that they'd arranged to pay a couple of neighbor kids who were looking for some extra cash.

There were only a couple days left before the shop's grand opening on Friday, the day before Valentine's Day—which reminded him that he should send something to Trent. Before he forgot, he paused in the hallway and pulled up Amazon on his phone. Thank goodness for two-day Prime delivery.

He ordered a Lego set and a giant Hershey Kiss in a red box, then selected Joy's address and submitted the order. Grant thought of the Valentine's boxes he'd made from shoeboxes in elementary school, and how he'd come home with dozens of small cards and pieces of candy. He wondered if Trent would be doing the same thing for his preschool class. It was the small things that were hard to miss, Grant thought.

He closed down the Amazon app just as a text came in. He didn't recognize the number, but it was signed *Taffy*.

He read the words a second time.

Hi Grant, I'm at the cemetery with Maurie, and I think she could really use a friend. You know, someone who knew her mom. If you can, come over. She's on the north side. I'm sitting in her car. She seemed to want time alone with her mom, but I don't like her being this alone and upset. —Taffy

Grant wrote back. *She's not exactly happy with me.*

Taffy's reply came a few seconds later. *She told me what happened, and I get your hesitation. But you knew her mom at least a little. You have that connection with Maurie, one I don't.*

Taffy was right, and he was done hesitating. *Ok,* he wrote, then pocketed his phone.

He climbed into his truck and headed along the frozen streets toward the Pine Valley Cemetery. His grandparents were buried in this cemetery, and yet Grant only made it here about once a year, with the rest of his family on Memorial Day weekend.

The single car idling in the parking lot was Maurie's. Grant could see that Taffy was sitting in the passenger seat. That was good because it meant that Maurie was still among the graves. He parked a few spots away from the car and shut off the ignition.

Taffy waved, then pointed out her front window. Within seconds he spotted Maurie, wearing a dark coat on the far north side.

Grant grabbed his coat from the back seat and climbed out of the truck. Before he could change his mind, he shrugged on his coat and started the trek across the cemetery. He was wearing his work boots, and they doubled as snow boots, easily cutting through the several inches of snow that blanketed the ground.

His footsteps were silent though, and he'd almost reached Maurie before she turned to see him.

He slowed, gauging the expression on her face. Her beautiful eyes were rimmed in red as if she'd been crying. It was the first time in days they'd been face to face, and Grant's heart felt like it was being slowly twisted from his chest.

Maurie merely stared at him, as if she couldn't believe he'd appeared in the cemetery.

"Hey," Grant said, shoving his hands into his coat pockets.

Maurie gave the slightest nod, then turned to the grave marker.

Grant waited for a couple of seconds, then walked toward the grave marker and stopped on the side of it, standing a few feet from Maurie. There was a small bouquet of flowers laying in the snow above the gravestone.

The inscription on the stone was simple. Name, birth and death dates. Nothing else. No decoration in the pale-gray stone. He read the dates. Maurie's mom had been forty-nine when she'd died. Not old at all.

He squatted and used the sleeve of his coat to brush away the snow from the edges of the stone. When he straightened, he felt Maurie's eyes on him. Several moments passed in silence, but for some reason, it wasn't awkward.

"I remember those green Christmas ornaments you guys always had on your tree," Grant said. "I told my mom about them, and she said that the tree was already green, so ornaments should be a different color."

Maurie said nothing, but he knew she was listening.

"But I thought the green was cool." He shrugged. "And the lights on your tree twinkled. That was pretty cool too."

"What did your mom say about the twinkling lights?" Maurie asked.

Relief shot through Grant. Maurie had finally spoken to him. "Nothing, because we had twinkling lights too."

The smallest smile touched Maurie's lips. The sight made Grant's heart ache. She was the most resilient person he knew.

"Were you the one who brought over the tin of Christmas sugar cookies?" she asked.

Grant had forgotten about that. His family had gotten so much stuff from neighbors that he didn't think his parents would notice some of it going missing. His mother probably wouldn't have minded him taking cookies, but he'd been afraid of his sister finding out. She was a merciless tease as a teenager.

"Yeah," Grant said.

Maurie gazed at him for a moment, and Grant held her gaze. He wished he knew what was going on inside her mind.

"I think you were the only one who cared about me in Pine Valley, Grant."

Grant wanted to argue, tell her that other people cared. But he couldn't think of a single one, except for maybe her mom in her twisted way. "I still care," he said in a quiet voice.

Maurie's eyes filled with tears, and she turned from him, gazing down at the gravestone.

He hated that she was in pain, and that some of it came from him.

As much as he wished he could pull her into his arms and comfort her, he didn't move. Maurie's shoulders were tense, and he didn't want to make things worse.

She wiped at her cheeks, then sniffled. "I'm pretty sure that Taffy told you to come, but I'm glad you did."

Grant took a step closer. "If I can help, I will."

"I know." Maurie took a stuttering breath. "But there are some things no one can help with."

"Do you really think that?" he asked. When she nodded, he continued, "Maybe I can't fix things, and we certainly can't go back in time. But don't you think it's better to face life's challenges with someone else—with someone who cares?"

Maurie didn't answer. And maybe she didn't need to. Grant might have crossed the line, and now wasn't the time to discuss what had been building between them. For now, Maurie's visit to her mother's grave was an important process for her to go through. Grant couldn't expect anything else.

He took another step closer. "I think you're a brave woman, Maurie Ledbetter. You've overcome more than most people do in their entire lifetimes. You've built a successful business, you have good people in your life, and you're kind and generous."

Maurie closed her eyes.

Grant bent close to kiss her cheek. She didn't pull away, but she didn't turn toward him either.

He stepped back. "I hope you can find the peace and happiness you deserve, because if there's anyone who deserves it, it's you."

Maurie opened her eyes and fiddled with the zipper on her coat as the wind kicked up, stirring her dark hair.

"Don't stay out here too long," Grant said.

She gave him the slightest of nods, although her eyes still hadn't connected with his.

Grant walked away, moving through the snow the same way he'd come. Maurie's car was still idling in the parking lot with Taffy inside. She lifted a hand in greeting as he continued to his truck. He waved back. There was nothing to discuss with Taffy, and he didn't want to put her in between him and Maurie anyway.

So Grant returned to Maurie's house and finished the cleanup. Taffy and Maurie must have gone straight from the cemetery to the shop because they hadn't returned to the house by the time he'd loaded all his tools into his truck. It was late afternoon now, and he'd checked and rechecked all of his work.

Maybe he could run by the store, see if they needed help tonight since tomorrow was the grand opening. He could let Maurie know he was completely finished with her house. Or maybe he should let things stand where they were.

Outside, he was slipping off his tool belt and setting it on the passenger seat of his truck when his phone rang. *Joy.*

"Hello?" he answered.

Joy's breathless voice came on. "Stone's taking me on a surprise Valentine's getaway," she said. "Can you pick up Trent for the weekend?"

Grant wasn't sure if he heard right. Having Trent so soon after his sick visit was unexpected. Grant had been counting down the days until the first week of March and Trent's spring break. "This weekend?" It was Thursday night.

"Yes," she said. "We're leaving first thing in the morning, so tonight would be best. I don't want to have to deal with him in the morning."

Grant's mind spun. "Uh, I need to switch to the SUV, and then I can head over."

"Great," Joy said. "He needs to be home by Sunday night, six sharp. I want to make sure he gets a good dinner in him and a full night's sleep for school the next day."

"All right." Although it was completely last minute, he wasn't going to complain. He didn't have much going on over the weekend. He'd considered starting the next job he was booked for early, but he could put that off until Monday.

"Oh, I hope you didn't have Valentine's plans," Joy said in a completely unsympathetic voice. "Well, if you do, I guess Trent will be a third wheel."

"I . . ." Even before things fell apart with Maurie, he had known she'd be busy with her store opening. Valentine's Day was Saturday, but it wasn't like he was dating anyone. Anymore. "Trent is welcome at my place. I'm on my way."

By the time Grant arrived at Joy's house, he was met with a very sleepy Trent.

Grant had to admit that it was great to see his son fully healthy, unlike the last time. Grant pulled the little guy into a tight hug. Trent started to squirm and make fake choking sounds. "Lemme go, Daddy."

Daddy. Grant smiled at the name.

He glanced up at Joy and Stone—who was wearing a tuxedo of all things. Joy was equally decked out in a shimmering peach dress that left nothing to the imagination. They looked like they'd just returned from a high-dollar fundraiser gala, or maybe the Oscars.

He patiently listened as Joy explained the "homework" that Trent needed to do over the weekend; apparently preschoolers had homework. Who would have thought?

Grant nodded his agreement, then told Trent he'd give him a piggyback to the SUV. Trent eagerly hopped up on his back, and Grant gave him a ride to the SUV.

Once Trent was buckled in, Grant pulled out of the driveway. "Are you tired, buddy?" he asked.

"No," Trent said, then gave a giant yawn.

Grant tried not to laugh. "What did you have for dinner?"

"Spetti, and it was *green*," Trent said as if he was disgusted by it.

"Do you mean spinach fettuccini?"

"Yeah, that's what Mommy said." Trent yawned again.

Grant turned on the radio to a mellow station. He had no doubt that Trent would be falling asleep soon. "Well, I'm excited that you're coming to hang out with me for a few days."

"Me too," Trent said in a sleepy voice. "Where's Maurie?"

Grant should have expected that question, but it still felt like a punch in the gut.

"She's, uh, working at her store," he said lamely. "The store opens tomorrow, which means she's very busy."

"Can we see the store?" Trent asked, his voice more awake now. "Does she have lots of candy there?"

"I'm not sure," Grant said, wondering what all Maurie had told Trent.

Trent continued peppering questions for the next ten minutes, most of which Grant couldn't answer. When Trent fell asleep, Grant thought about how grateful he was for this stolen weekend with his son, and it almost made up for the disaster with Maurie. Almost.

Eighteen

Maurie stared at the fading darkness of the freshly painted blue walls of her bedroom. The winter sun was finally coming up. Without looking at her phone, she guessed it to be nearly 6:00 a.m. The grand opening for Every Occasion's storefront was in a few hours, and although she and Taffy had finished the final touches on the shop the night before, Maurie's thoughts were like a merry-go-round.

After seeing Grant at the cemetery, Maurie had gone through some serious introspection, along with talking things out with Taffy. Maurie knew that she didn't want to live life separately from the man she was falling in love with.

And it hadn't helped when she'd arrived home at 10:00 p.m. to find her house completely finished and cleaned up. Grant had left a handwritten note.

Maurie,

Sorry I missed you tonight. I hope everything meets with your satisfaction. If not, please let me know. Best of luck with the grand opening. Julie will be getting the invoice to you in

the next couple of weeks. No rush on payment.
Grant

Maurie had sunk into the kitchen chair after reading it the first time. Then she read it through again, this time paying attention to the strong, masculine handwriting that reminded her of the man behind the pen.

Now she closed her eyes against the encroaching dawn. Did she really blame Grant for calling the police that night? No. Dwelling on the what-ifs would only make her life harder. If she were truly to move forward, and use her shop's opening as a new beginning, then she'd have to face her feelings about Grant.

Because she did love him.

And she didn't want to lose him.

She knew too well what loss felt like.

Yet Grant's confession had taken her back to the vulnerable place that she also knew too well. And her first instinct had been to push Grant away, to pretend that what he'd told her didn't bother her, didn't hurt her. But it had. And that was okay. Yet now, she wanted to move on from the painful parts of her past.

She checked her cell. Nothing from Grant—not that she'd expected it.

It was 6:05 a.m., and time to start fresh.

She got out of bed, drew on her robe, and went into the kitchen. She made herself a steaming mug of hot cocoa and then sat down to write to Grant. She would write it all down and then drop off the letter at his place. This way she couldn't put it off any longer and she couldn't keep chickening out.

Dear Grant,
Life has given us both lemons, but from our first

encounters, you've been there for me. Somehow you saw something in me that I didn't even see in myself. I need to thank you for giving a lonely little girl something to look forward to. For being an example of goodness and simple kindness . . .

Maurie continued the letter, writing two full pages, until her eyes were burning with tears. She hoped that Grant would feel her sincerity, and even if he ultimately rejected their relationship, he still deserved a thank you and her heartfelt apology.

It was nearly 7:00 a.m. when she located an envelope and left the house. Taffy would be awake soon, and Maurie wanted to have the letter delivered before any other distractions arose. She drew on her coat, then bundled into her car. The steering wheel was freezing, but she pulled out of the drive anyway.

It took less than ten minutes to get to Grant's place, and when she pulled into his apartment complex, she gazed up at the windows that made up his place. She remembered how he'd let her sleep on the couch, and then how, on the following morning, she and Trent had spent one-on-one time together.

She climbed out of her car and crossed the parking lot, then walked to his apartment door. It was too early to knock, plus she'd said everything exactly how she wanted to say it in the letter. She wanted him to read it first. Then he could decide on the next move in their relationship, if he thought it was even salvageable.

Maurie tucked the letter into the seal of the door, near the bottom so that it wouldn't be so obvious if someone walked by and became curious. She hoped no one would take the letter. There was no sign of an impending storm, so she had good reason to believe that Grant would probably find it within the next hour. She didn't know what his next job would be, but she didn't imagine him sleeping in too long on a Friday.

Maurie turned away from the apartment and hurried back to her car. It was still warm inside, and she started the ignition. Nerves jangled through her as she drove away from the apartment complex, but she knew she'd done the right thing.

Now she'd have to rush to get showered and presentable for the grand opening.

Her heart pounded at the thought of him reading her words, reading her own confession, but she continued to drive back home. With every minute that passed, she imagined Grant opening the door and finding her letter. Would he read it inside his place, or maybe while sitting in his truck? Would he call her or text her? Or maybe he'd do nothing.

An hour later, she and Taffy loaded the car with last-minute items, then drove to Main Street Café to pick up the ten dozen donuts they'd ordered. When they came out of the café, Maurie could see about fifteen people lined up in front of her new shop.

"Are they here for us?" Taffy asked.

"I think so." Maurie couldn't imagine why else a group of people would be standing out in the cold.

"Oh. My. Heck!" Taffy continued. "My fliers worked!"

Maurie laughed at that as a thrill buzzed through her. The small crowd looked to be a mixture of locals as well as the touristy ski bunnies. "Let's go. We're opening early."

Taffy squealed and climbed into the car.

Maurie headed down the road and drove to the rear parking lot. Half of the parking spaces were already filled, and she parked closest to the rear door of the shop. They carried in the donuts, and even though it was almost an hour before the official opening, Maurie wasn't going to let potential customers stay out in the cold.

"I'll get the hot-cocoa machine heating up," Maurie said. "Can you arrange the donuts, then we'll open the doors?"

Taffy flipped on all the lights, then made quick work of setting out the first couple boxes of donuts on the table they'd decorated with all things Valentine's. Next, Taffy headed to the front door and unlocked it. "Come in, come in! Free hot chocolate and donuts. And don't miss out on the fifty-percent-off coupon we're offering today. Valentine's Day is tomorrow, folks!"

Maurie could only grin at Taffy's enthusiasm. Maurie crossed to the entrance and greeted the customers too, one by one, introducing herself and explaining what her store was all about.

"The place is gorgeous," one woman said. "I'll have to get my mother down here. She's going to love it."

Maurie had never smiled so much. Even local business owners stopped by, introducing themselves and complimenting the place. Around mid-morning, the realtor Jeff Finch stepped inside.

"I love it," he declared, and he enthusiastically shook both Maurie's and Taffy's hands. He gave Maurie a box of chocolate truffles. "Something for you, although you're probably stocked to the gills with stuff like this."

"I love truffles," Maurie said. "Thank you."

Jeff smiled, then became caught up in a conversation with another customer.

Maurie surveyed the customers with pride. Several sales had already been made, and she'd helped a few customers put together custom orders. An older couple was poring through her catalog of gift-basket ideas.

Everyone who stopped in seemed friendly and excited for the new store addition to Pine Valley. Maurie helped herself to a donut and had her own cup of hot cocoa—or two.

The time sped by, and soon it was nearly 2:00 p.m. Maurie had been so busy that she hadn't been worrying about her letter to Grant and what he thought of it. She was grateful for the business. The customers seemed to come in spurts now, so during a quieter interval, Maurie told Taffy, "You can take a break if you want. Why don't you grab us a couple of sandwiches from the café down the street?"

"Ah, so my break is getting *you* food?" Taffy laughed.

Maurie smirked. "Don't tell me you're not hungry."

"I'm starving," Taffy said.

"Okay then. Ham and Swiss on country sourdough sounds good."

Taffy nodded. "I'll get the same for me."

"And maybe a Diet Coke."

"Got it," Taffy said. "Should I get more donuts?"

There was only one box left, a testament to the number of visitors they'd had. It was amazing, really. "Maybe one more box," Maurie folded the two empty boxes on the table. She checked the contents of the hot-cocoa machine.

"Uh, Maurie," Taffy said, "you might want to change your lunch order."

Maurie looked over to see a man opening the shop door. Her pulse jumped. His tall form dominated the doorway as he stepped inside. Grant's lake blue eyes focused on her. He held the hand of a little boy—Trent—who carried a large sack with *Main Street Café* printed on the side.

In Grant's other hand was a bouquet of red roses.

"Grant," Maurie said, not realizing she'd spoken out loud until Trent spoke.

"It's Maurie, Daddy," Trent said, tugging on his dad's hand.

"Yeah," Grant said; his blue eyes studied Maurie's. His expression was wary, perhaps even vulnerable. He wore a black sweater that only emphasized his broad shoulders, and his jeans were well-worn, faded. She guessed he hadn't shaved that morning, because stubble shadowed his face.

"Look at the donuts," Trent blurted.

One of the customers asked Maurie a question, but Taffy intervened.

Trent tugged his dad across the store space toward the refreshment table, where Maurie stood. Her breath went shallow. Grant was here, and he'd brought flowers. Were the flowers to celebrate the grand opening, or were they more . . . personal? Had he read her letter? He must have. Did she dare believe that he wasn't here just because of the grand opening or the fact that Trent was really excited about donuts?

Grant glanced down at his eager son reaching for a donut. "You need to ask, Trent."

"Can kids have the donuts?" Trent asked, turning his pleading eyes to Maurie.

"Of course," Maurie said, a smile blooming on her face as her pulse raced. She met Grant's gaze. "If it's okay with your dad."

"Sure," Grant said, not taking his gaze from Maurie's.

"Yippee!" Trent said, and he set the sack he carried on the table, then grabbed for a donut.

"Keep the napkin with it," Grant said. "And try not to make a mess." His tone of voice wasn't a reprimand, but full of affection.

A warm shiver shot through Maurie as Grant took a step closer to her. She caught his clean, spicy scent. She wanted to close her eyes, to breathe him in. But there were other customers in the store, not to mention his kid.

"Did you get my letter?" she whispered.

His mouth curved slowly. "I did."

Maurie's knees felt all watery.

"Daddy, can I have hot chocolate too?" Trent asked.

Grant glanced down at his son. "Sure. And I can promise, it's really good."

"I can fix you a cup." Taffy's voice came from somewhere—Maurie wasn't really sure, because Grant had taken another step closer so she had to tilt her head to meet his gaze.

"We brought you lunch," Trent continued, "and my daddy got you flowers for Valentine's."

Grant smiled, and Maurie's heart hitched.

"He's right," Grant said.

"Lunch *and* flowers?" Maurie said, returning his smile. "How did I get so lucky?"

Grant reached for her hand, and the touch of his warm fingers made goose bumps skitter along her skin. There was no doubt. He was here for her.

"Aren't you going to give her the flowers, Daddy?"

Grant's chuckle was low, and Maurie's cheeks went hot.

His fingers caressed hers, and Maurie thought she might melt right there on the spot.

"So . . ." Grant said in a low voice. "I was wondering if you had plans tomorrow—for Valentine's Day. I mean, after the shop closes. So I guess it would be night."

"I don't have plans," Maurie said in a soft voice.

"I have Trent for the weekend, so it would be the three of us." He was watching her carefully, as if to gauge her reaction. "If Taffy wants to come too, then it would be four of us."

"Unless you're too tired," Trent piped up. "My dad said you've been working a lot, and that opening a store is a super big job."

"Well," Maurie said, looking down at Trent, if only to get a break from Grant's intense gaze and the way it was making her pulse rate double, "I *have* been working really hard."

Grant squeezed her hand, and she met his gaze again.

"But I'd love to go out with both of you," she said.

He grinned, and Trent said, "Yippee."

Maurie smiled. Today she'd officially broken whatever smiling record she had.

"And these are for you, in case you were wondering." Grant winked and held up the roses.

Maurie laughed and took the bouquet with her free hand. "Thank you. They're beautiful." She breathed them in, closing her eyes for a moment.

"Does that mean she likes them, Daddy?" Trent said.

"Yes, I believe it does," Grant said in an amused tone.

Maurie opened her eyes, only to be caught up in Grant's intense gaze again. Taffy's voice murmured in the background while she chatted with a customer, and Trent might have asked another question, or a dozen. But Maurie felt herself unable to stop staring at the man about whom she hadn't been able to stop thinking for weeks, perhaps years.

Maurie placed her hand on his chest, lifted up on her toes, and kissed his cheek.

Grant raised his brows as she drew away, then he took the roses from her and set them on the refreshment table. Next he slipped his hands around her waist, and he leaned down. Close enough to kiss her. Which he did. On the mouth. And Maurie kissed him back, even though they were standing in the middle of her shop, surrounded by people. Despite the public setting, he pulled her closer and deepened the kiss.

Kissing Grant was so much better than the best hot cocoa, a store full of customers, or beautiful flowers.

When Grant lifted his head, he was grinning, she was blushing, and the customers were clapping.

Nineteen

"Go home and get ready," Taffy told Maurie when the final customer had left the shop. "I can close up."

It was Saturday around 6:00 p.m. Business at the shop had been brisk most of the day, and they had stayed open a little longer to help a few desperate husbands find the perfect valentines for their wives.

Maurie didn't want to leave Taffy to close up everything, but the offer was tempting. Since Grant's surprise arrival the day before, they'd been texting each other. Mostly flirting, if Maurie were to describe it. Grant had also shared some funny things about Trent, who apparently kept asking when Maurie would be done working.

"You can borrow my silver stilettos if you want," Taffy continued. "You know you want to."

"They're too fancy," Maurie told her friend. "He said we're going to some barbecue place. He couldn't get reservations at the lodge—besides, it's not really a place to take little kids."

Taffy shrugged. "It's Valentine's! Be a little daring and

dress up. Knock the boots off that man. Plus, Brandon wasn't tall enough for you to wear heels."

Maurie laughed. Then she sobered. "What about you? Are you sure you don't want to come? I mean, we'll have a little kid with us, so it's not like we're going for the romance."

"I have a date with Netflix," Taffy said. "Besides, I plan to eat at least half the box of those truffles Jeff Finch brought over yesterday."

Maurie had already tried one, or three, and they were delicious. "Help yourself. But I'm serious about the invite."

Taffy smiled. "I know you are, and I love you for it. But you go be a happy little family with Grant Shelton. I'll bask in the warmth that the three of you radiate."

It was a sweet comment, but it also gave Maurie pause. Being in a relationship with Grant wasn't just about the two of them. It would always include his son, and to some extent, issues with his ex-wife. Maurie was surprised at how it didn't bother her. Yes, things were more complicated, but Maurie adored Trent.

She loved his questions and innocent curiosity. It wasn't hard to see why Grant centered his whole world around his son. And now that world included her too.

"Okay, if you're sure," Maurie told Taffy. "Thank you." She hugged her best friend and only employee, then grabbed her coat from the back room.

The cold air didn't even feel cold as Maurie stepped outside. She'd opened the store that morning, so Taffy had driven over later. As Maurie headed home, she marveled at the changes in the past few weeks of her life. She owned a home and a store, and Grant Shelton was in her life.

She hadn't known it was possible to feel so much happiness in a single moment of time. Maybe she would wear the silver stilettos. Grant was definitely tall enough that she wouldn't tower over him. She had a couple of dressy outfits she could wear. Her navy dress with the long bell sleeves and flirty skirt might work.

By the time she got home, her pulse was drumming in anticipation. She supposed that she and Grant were officially a couple and this would be their first outing as such. And Trent's presence would only make things more concrete.

After a quick shower, keeping her hair dry, Maurie changed into the navy dress. It was nice, but not too dressy. Next she put on some silver hoop earrings and a silver heart necklace that her foster mom, Gladys, had given her. Maurie made her way to Taffy's bedroom.

Maurie had to do some digging to find the silver stilettos, and once she had them on, she realized she needed to practice walking in them. So she went into the kitchen and walked around the table a few times.

Next, Maurie pulled her hair into a twist, then used bobby pins to hold it in place. She didn't want to go too heavy on the makeup, so she used a pale eye shadow, then mascara and lip gloss.

Satisfied, she was ready a full fifteen minutes before Grant was due to arrive.

She walked around the house, appreciating all of Grant's work. He was everywhere. The only thing left was replacing the carpet. When headlights flashed across the window, Maurie moved to the front door. She didn't open it yet, but waited for Grant to come and knock.

First, she heard Trent's little voice: "Is Taffy her sister? Is that why she lives here too?"

"No, they're friends," Grant said in his deeper voice.

Maurie smiled.

"Can I push the doorbell?" Trent asked.

"Sure."

The doorbell rang, and Maurie stifled a laugh. She grabbed her purse with her phone, then answered the door.

Standing on her porch was Grant, dressed in a blazer, button-down shirt, and dark pants. No tie. Next to him, Trent stood wearing a small blazer that was just his size, and he wore a bowtie. He looked adorable. And Grant, well, he looked delicious.

She opened the screen door and stepped out onto the porch. "How did I get so lucky as to have two handsome men on my doorstep?"

"I'm a kid, not a man!" Trent pronounced.

Maurie laughed. "Well, you look very grown up, Trent."

The young boy stepped forward and wrapped his arms about her legs.

Maurie was startled by his easy affection, but she loved it too. She bent and hugged him back, then she looked up at Grant. He was gazing at her like . . . well, like a man gazes at a woman he is serious about.

She straightened and met Grant's blue gaze. She was nearly his height with her stilettos on. "Hey."

"Hey." Grant stepped close and rested his hand on her hip as he leaned in and kissed her cheek. He lingered, not moving back just yet. "You look stunning," he said in a soft voice next to her ear.

"You don't look so bad yourself," Maurie said because she wanted to dispel some of the emotions she was feeling. Everywhere he touched, her skin burned.

Grant smiled, still lingering, so that she felt his warm breath against her neck.

"I like your shoes," he said.

"They're Taffy's," Maurie answered.

"I still like them." He lowered his hand and grasped hers, threading their fingers together.

It might be below freezing outside, but Maurie wasn't cold in the least. She didn't bother to lock the front door because Taffy would be home any minute. Besides, it was Pine Valley.

"Daddy didn't want to bring the truck," Trent said. "Because it's dirty. It's a work truck."

"Yes," Maurie said. "I can understand that." She squeezed Grant's hand, and he squeezed back.

"Daddy says we have to open your door," Trent continued.

Maurie wanted to laugh, but she could hear the seriousness of Trent's voice. "That would be very nice of you."

Trent ran ahead, and Grant called out, "Careful. It could be icy."

"I won't fall," Trent shouted. He ran around the front of the SUV and tugged open the door with a grunt.

"You're raising quite the gentleman, Mr. Shelton," Maurie said in a quiet voice.

"It will keep him busy tonight," Grant said. "Sorry it can't be just us."

"Don't apologize," Maurie said. "Trent's a great kid. I'm getting two for the price of one."

They reached the passenger door, and Maurie climbed into the car. "Thank you, Trent."

"You're welcome," Trent said before he used both hands to shut the door.

Grant then opened the back door and ushered Trent into the back seat. Once they were all seated, Grant backed out of the driveway, and they drove outside of Pine Valley to Rick's BBQ.

Trent talked most of the way, and Grant indulged his conversation. Maurie found herself smiling most of the time, and she also relished the fact that Grant held her hand on the drive.

When Grant pulled into the parking lot of the restaurant, he had to park in the far corner because there were so many cars.

"Good thing I made a reservation," Grant said, turning to look at Maurie. "Have you eaten here before?"

"I don't think so," Maurie said. "My mom and I didn't go out much. At least not together."

Trent must have unbuckled his seatbelt, because he suddenly popped his head between the two of them. "Maurie, do you like my daddy?"

Maurie blinked. "Um, yes, I do like your dad."

Trent nodded. "That's what I thought. I love barbeque. Do you?"

"It's great," Maurie said.

"Speaking of great, let's go inside," Grant said, amusement in his tone.

Trent spoke up from the back seat. "She has to wait for us to open her door, right, Daddy?"

"Right," Grant confirmed.

So Maurie waited while the two males opened her door, and as they walked to the restaurant, Grant leaned in close and whispered, "So you like me, huh?"

Maurie smiled. "I do."

Grant linked their fingers, and Maurie's heart squeezed.

A group of people spilled out of the restaurant door, their laughter and conversation superseding any reply that Grant might have given.

One of the men kept the door open, holding it for Maurie's group.

"Thank you," Trent said to the man, who smiled down at him. "Guys can open doors for other guys, huh, Dad?"

"Yep," Grant said, then winked at Maurie. He kept hold of her hand as he gave his name to the hostess for their reservation.

The hostess led them right to a booth, and as they walked past the other tables, Maurie felt more than one pair of eyes on them. Surely some of these people knew Grant. And now they would see them together.

Maurie's heart soared to think that Grant was still holding her hand, in front of all these people.

She slid into the booth, and Trent said he wanted to sit by both of them, so he sat in the middle. Maurie was flattered. Trent propped his elbows on the table and said, "Is there a kid's menu?"

The hostess smiled and handed over a large rectangular menu that could be colored on. She also set down three crayons. "Your server will be here shortly to take your drink order."

Well, this was certainly a unique Valentine's date, with a kid between her and her date, but Maurie wouldn't trade it for anything.

"Can I get soda, Daddy?" Trent asked.

Grant glanced at Maurie, then said, "Sure, but no refills. So why don't you get water too in case you're still thirsty."

Trent pushed out his lower lip as if he was considering whether or not to be upset by this.

"I'm going to get water," Maurie said.

Trent turned his blue gaze toward her. "You are? Do you get lemons in your water? My mommy does."

"Sometimes," Maurie said with a smile.

Trent shrugged. "Okay, I'll get water. Then we can be the same."

"Sounds like a plan." Maurie held back a laugh. When she met Grant's gaze, she saw appreciation and amusement there.

Grant's phone rang from where he'd set it on the table. He made a move to silence it, but Trent saw the screen. "Joy," Trent said. "That's Mommy!"

Grant hid a grimace and said, "Yeah, we'll call her later."

But Trent was grabbing for the phone, and before Grant could stop him, he answered. "Hi, Mommy."

Grant rubbed at his face, and Maurie mouthed to him, "It's okay."

This Valentine's date was definitely new, uncharted territory.

Twenty

Grant knew that Joy wasn't calling to wish him, or Trent, a happy Valentine's Day. And it was too early for a bedtime call. A phone call this early in the evening meant that she had an agenda. Trent was chatting happily with her, and Grant stole a couple of glances at Maurie. He wished they were sitting right next to each other so he could assure her that this phone call wasn't planned.

The waitress came, and Grant held up his hand to request a few more minutes. He knew by experience that Trent's food preferences changed quickly, and Grant didn't want to order the wrong thing. He wanted to avoid any pouting from Trent, especially on a night out with Maurie. Trent was enamored of her, which was a great thing, but he was also a four-year-old kid who could make or break an evening.

"Mommy wants to talk to you," Trent announced, holding out the phone.

Grant's stomach knotted. He hadn't been following Trent's chatter, so he wasn't sure what all had been said. He'd keep the conversation short.

"Hi, Joy," he said into the phone.

"Trent says you're at a restaurant and that your girlfriend's with you," Joy said, her tone accusatory.

Grant couldn't fathom why she thought she had the right to be so hostile about Maurie. Had Trent said *girlfriend*, or were those Joy's words? "That's right," Grant said. "Is there something you forgot to tell me about Trent?"

"I called because there are serious issues with that woman you're dating," Joy said in a hard tone, "and I don't want Trent around her."

Grant opened his mouth, but had no reply. He was stunned. Glancing at Maurie to see that she and Trent were busy coloring on his menu, he said into the phone, "Hang on, I need to find a place to talk."

Then he said to Maurie and Trent, "I'll be back in a couple of minutes."

Maurie's gaze looked concerned, but there wasn't any other choice. If he told Joy he'd call her later, he'd just be focused on another dreaded phone call.

He hurried out of the restaurant, and although it was cold outside and he had no coat, he didn't feel cold.

"Are you still there?" he said into the phone.

"Oh, I'm still here, Grant," Joy said. "I'll always be here, especially when it concerns my son."

Grant rubbed at his temple. He hated when Joy said *my son*, effectively cutting him out of the equation.

"Trent told me all about your girlfriend," Joy said, "and so I did a little digging."

Grant had no words.

"Bottom line, she's not fit to be around Trent," Joy said. "If you aren't willing to break things off, then I'm going to have the custody arrangement appealed—"

"Can you explain where the hell you are coming up with

your accusations?" Grant said, cutting her off. "There's nothing wrong with Maurie. I think you need to look at your own decisions before you point fingers."

"My mother isn't a convict," Joy spat out. "And I never lived in a druggie house and did who-knows-what with who-knows-who."

Grant's mind reeled. This was about Maurie's *mother*? He had to calm down, because right now, he wanted to hit something. Hard. And he was standing in the parking lot of a public restaurant, with Maurie and Trent waiting for him inside. He squeezed his eyes shut and pulled all the calm he could muster. "I knew Maurie as a kid. She lived down the block from me. When her mom went to jail, Maurie went into foster care. She never had contact with her mom again, and Maurie is *nothing* like her mother."

"Yet," Joy said.

The single word was so unfair, so judgmental.

"She's not," Grant said. "Maurie was homeschooled, and yes, her mom was a screw-up. But Maurie's not. She went to college, and she just opened a business in Pine Valley."

"Wow," Joy said. "I should give her a gold star. And you too. Was Maurie your teenage crush?"

At this, Grant hesitated. Joy had a gift of twisting his words, so he had to tread carefully. "We never dated."

Joy scoffed. "That's not very reassuring. All I know is that this woman is now in Trent's life, and that's what I have an issue with."

"I can't have this conversation right now," Grant said. "You don't know Maurie, and you can't pass judgment on her like this. It's completely insane."

Joy laughed. "Oh, pull the *insanity* card. That's convenient. I find it really interesting that you've always sat on your high horse, looking down at me, when in fact, you've apparently known Maurie for a long time. Do you know how that makes me feel to find out that you've gone back to your old girlfriend?"

"She's not my old girlfriend," Grant said. "And even if she were, that has nothing to do with this conversation. Maurie is a good person. The most decent woman that I know." It might be a low blow to Joy, but it was the truth. "If you need to appeal the custody agreement, then that's your choice, but I'm not dumping Maurie."

Joy went silent, but Grant knew she was just fuming.

Before she could spew any more bitterness, he said, "I'm hanging up now. You're on a weekend trip with Stone, and I have a dinner to get back to. We can talk when I bring Trent back on Sunday night. If you want updates on Trent, I'm happy to text you. But I won't be answering any of your calls."

Grant hung up and made good on his promise by turning off his phone. Then he paced the parking lot for a few more minutes. He had to cool down. Let his heart rate settle. Let the anger dissipate. He couldn't imagine Joy being jealous of Maurie, but he didn't know where all of her hatred was coming from. Maybe, just maybe, Joy had panicked, but it was pretty extreme to do all that research on Maurie.

His sister, Julie, had told him that she thought Joy was a narcissist. Grant had looked up the diagnosis once, and Joy had met eight of the ten requirements. He could hear Julie's voice in his head telling him that Joy would be angry if she thought he was moving on from her. Despite their divorce, Joy didn't want *him* to be happy.

It made a strange kind of sense, Grant had to admit. But it was still pathetic.

He went back into the restaurant. As he approached the table, he saw that an appetizer of loaded baked-potato skins had been delivered.

"What's this?" Grant asked, hoping his voice sounded lighthearted.

"Skins!" Trent said.

Grant met Maurie's questioning gaze. "Sounds good. I love 'skins.'"

Maurie smiled. "Great, because we weren't sure what you wanted to order. Trent said your favorite food is coffee, but I thought we'd wait until you returned."

Grant slid into the bench on Maurie's side, so he could sit by her. She looked surprised and scooted over. And luckily, Trent was so excited about the 'skins' that he didn't notice. "Sorry for the wait," he said, and he reached for her hand.

Her fingers interlocked with his, and the warmth of her hand was already making him feel better. Joy was feeling farther away by the minute.

"See my picture?" Trent said, holding up his menu.

Grant couldn't quite make out what Trent had drawn. It looked like a huge blue scribble, sort of a cross between a dinosaur and a truck. "What's his name?" he asked, using the trick of asking a question about his son's art to get him to say what it was.

"It's Brady the dinosaur," Trent said.

Ah. Grant had been half right. "Brady looks like a strong dinosaur." He felt the beginnings of a headache, which wasn't too surprising after the fight he'd had with Joy. He reached for a potato skin and bit into it.

"Do you like the skin, Daddy?" Trent asked, watching him carefully.

Grant smiled. "It's delicious."

Trent nodded happily, then picked up another crayon and returned to his coloring. Apparently Brady the Dinosaur was going to be blue *and* red.

Maurie had been quiet, but he also knew she was

observant. So he wasn't surprised when she whispered, "Is everything okay?"

Grant met her gaze. Why couldn't he have skipped the whole Joy stage and gone right to Maurie? Of course, then he wouldn't have Trent.

"It will be," Grant said, rubbing his thumb over her fingers. "I'm glad you're here."

Maurie smiled, but the concern was still evident in her eyes. "I'm glad too."

She was an amazing woman. Joy didn't even come close to a woman like Maurie.

"You're a great dad," Maurie continued in a soft voice. "Trent thinks you walk on water. Which I have to agree with." She squeezed his hand.

Grant exhaled. "If you keep complimenting me, I'm going to have to kiss you in front of everyone."

Her brows lifted. "Is that a threat?" she teased.

"Have you had a chance to decide?" another voice said.

Grant looked up to see a waitress. She was perhaps in her fifties and wore dark pants and a pink shirt—the standard server uniform here. Her nametag read *Sylvia*, and she looked a bit harried. The place was busy, and surely they'd taken more than their fair share of time. "I'll have the half order of ribs," he said.

Maurie ordered the cobb salad, and Trent ordered the kids' grilled-cheese meal.

"Great," Sylvia said, then she hesitated. "We've opened up the dancing on the other side of the restaurant for Valentine's. Usually we only have the floor open on Monday nights for Western night."

"Okay, great, thanks," Grant said.

As Sylvia walked away, Trent said, "You should dance with Maurie, Daddy."

Grant looked at Maurie. "Do you want to dance?"

Maurie's cheeks stained red. "Um, no, thank you though." She looked at Trent, pointedly ignoring Grant's gaze. "Thanks for thinking of me, but I don't dance."

"It's not line dancing or anything," Grant said. He could see where the dancing was underway, and there were a handful of couples swaying slowly to the music. "Just slow stuff."

"I don't think so."

Grant could see that she was truly uncomfortable. Maybe it was the public restaurant setting. "Okay. I think we should play Guess What Animal I'm Making."

Trent clapped his hands. "Can I go first?"

Grant chuckled. "Of course."

"We have to make animals with our hands and then guess what it is," Trent told Maurie.

"Sounds fun," she said.

Grant loved how she was always so positive around Trent.

Whatever Trent was making with his hands didn't resemble any animal that Grant could think of, which was often the case with this game. "A bear?" Grant guessed.

"No," Trent said, then turned his hopeful eyes to Maurie.

"A lion?" Maurie said.

Apparently her guess wasn't any better, because Trent said, "Nope. It's a wolf!"

"That was my next guess," Grant said.

Trent laughed. "You always say that!"

Maurie lifted her brows. "Okay, can I have a turn?"

They played the game until their meals were delivered. As Grant ate, he realized it had been at least fifteen minutes since he'd thought of Joy. Very good progress.

After they finished eating and Grant paid the bill, they

left the restaurant and headed for the car. Trent jumped ahead of them. "Stay by me," Grant said, grabbing for his hand. "No running in a parking lot, remember."

Trent latched onto Grant's hand, then reached for Maurie's as well.

Maurie looked surprised, then she smiled over at Grant.

It seemed Trent was just as taken with Maurie as Grant was.

"Can I open Maurie's door?" Trent asked.

"Sure, buddy." Grant used his key fob to unlock the doors, and Trent heaved open the passenger door.

"Thanks, Trent," Maurie said, and she ruffled the kid's hair as she got in.

Trent smoothed his hair back down, but he was smiling as he climbed into the back. When Grant settled into the driver's seat and started the engine, Trent asked, "Are we going home now?"

"We need to take Maurie home first," Grant said.

"But I want to show her my new toothbrush," Trent said. "It has a battery and shakes."

"We could show her another time," Grant said. "It's almost your bedtime."

"You could take me to get my car," Maurie said, "and I could come over really quick."

Before Grant could answer, Trent said, "Can she, Daddy? Please?"

Grant wasn't going to tell Maurie *not* to come over. He glanced at her. "If you're sure."

"Yep."

Twenty-One

Maurie sat in the dark in her car for a couple of minutes before climbing out and knocking on Grant's door. Had she bulldozed her way into coming over? Had Grant wanted to call it an evening? Even though Trent was a part of everything, she felt that Grant had been trying to cut the date short.

Not that they'd planned to go to a movie or anything, and it was a bit late for a four-year-old. Still, Maurie had noticed Grant's mood change when he'd come back into the restaurant after talking to Joy outside. Maurie still didn't know what they'd talked about, but Grant's face had been pale when he'd returned.

Maurie hated that his ex-wife could still affect him emotionally. She was at a loss of how to help him, but she supposed divorces were complicated enough without trying to work out sharing custody of children.

She hoped that Grant trusted her enough to talk to her about whatever he was going through.

The car was getting cold, so she opened the door and climbed out. The lights were on in Grant's apartment, and

Maurie smiled as she thought of how excited Trent was about the simple things in life. Like a new toothbrush. She tried not to compare Trent's life to her own childhood. It was a never-ending, dark tunnel whenever she started the comparison game.

She needed to consider herself blessed to have a man like Grant to date, and Trent was just an added bonus.

After she knocked, she heard Trent yell something, then the lower tone of Grant's voice. By the time the two of them opened the door, Maurie was smiling. They were adorable together.

"Hi." She was relieved to see that some of the shadows beneath Grant's eyes had faded. He'd also taken off his blazer and rolled up the sleeves of his button-down shirt. Maurie couldn't decide which look she liked best. All of his looks were great.

Trent was wearing *Incredibles* pajamas with giant *Cars* slippers.

"Come in," Grant said, and she stepped past him.

"See my toothbrush?" Trent held it up, as if he'd been waiting for her knock on the door.

Grant shut the door, and Maurie bent to examine the toothbrush. It was one of those automatic ones.

"Watch." Trent flicked the small on-off button, and the toothbrush whirred to life. "Stone says that it will keep the cavity bugs away."

"Definitely," Maurie said.

"Do you want to see me brush my teeth?" Trent asked.

Maurie shouldn't have been surprised. The question was so Trent-like.

"Uh, you don't have to," Grant told her.

She glanced up at him from her crouched position. "It's okay. I can watch."

So the three of them crowded into the bathroom while Trent demonstrated brushing his teeth. Maurie kept in her laughter. And Grant did a pretty good job at distracting her when he rested his hand on the back of her neck and slowly ran his thumb over her skin.

His touch gave her goose bumps. And she could smell his clean, spicy scent. Maybe she should have danced with him at the restaurant. No . . . not with everyone watching. She was proud of herself for walking in her stilettos. Dancing would have been another matter.

When Trent finished, he wiped his mouth on a towel, then said, "See how clean my teeth are? No cavity bugs."

"I don't see any, do you, Grant?" Maurie said.

"I don't either." Grant's tone was amused, and the three of them in the bathroom was feeling a bit too cozy.

"Can you read me a story?" Trent asked, looking up at Maurie with those pleading blue eyes.

Her heart felt like it would burst. How could she say no?

"Trent, I don't think—" Grant started to say.

"It's okay," Maurie said. "I'd love to."

Trent grinned, then bounded out of the bathroom. "I'll get the book."

Grant grasped her hand before she could leave the bathroom. "Are you sure, Maurie?"

She gazed into his equally blue eyes. "I'm sure, but are *you* sure?"

His brows lifted. "What do you mean?"

"Well, it's all very . . ." She hesitated. "Family-like. And we're sort of newly dating. If it's too much, then I can tell him I need to leave."

"Don't leave." Grant moved his hands to her waist. "And I'm more than happy that Trent likes you." He leaned close and lowered his voice. "I'm *really* happy about it."

Maurie placed her hands on his chest. Was he going to kiss her with his kid so close by? Trent could see them at any moment. "Okay, then let's go read a story."

Grant smiled and lowered his face to hers. His lips had barely brushed hers when Trent called out, "Found it!"

Maurie tugged Grant closer anyway, and although their kiss was way too brief, her skin buzzed with the contact. They walked hand in hand into Trent's bedroom, and Maurie was presented with a book on trains. She settled on the bed next to Trent, and Grant perched on the edge of the bed. With the smaller twin size, there wasn't room for the three of them.

Maurie cleared her throat and began to read the story. Grant was watching her with amusement but she forged ahead. She wouldn't consider herself a great storyteller, but Trent was easy to read to. And even though it was apparent he had the book memorized, he was so enthusiastic about the story that it made Maurie's heart swell.

She'd never felt so . . . fulfilled. She didn't know how else to describe it. Sitting in this bedroom with Trent and Grant while they read about a "family" of trains made her realize that the simple things in life could be the best things.

When she came to the last page, Trent wouldn't let her close the book. "Read it again," he begged.

"Not tonight," Grant said, his voice firm. "We have a fun day planned tomorrow, and I don't want you tired."

Trent's eyes lit up. "Can Maurie come too?"

"I'll ask her," Grant said. "But you need to go to sleep now." He rose and took the book from Trent's grasp.

"Okay," Trent said, his tone dejected.

"Good night, Trent," Maurie said, rising as well. She didn't want to be the cause of Trent not listening to his father.

She left the room while Grant tucked him in and gave him a few more instructions. In the living room, Maurie stayed standing. She felt like she was too formally dressed to lounge on the couch, and she hoped that she could find out from Grant why he'd been so upset over the phone call with his ex.

A few minutes later, Grant came out of Trent's bedroom and shut the door with a quiet click.

Maurie turned to face him as he walked into the living room. He didn't say anything, but grasped her hand and drew her into the kitchen. "Trent's kind of demanding," Grant said in a soft voice, pulling her toward him and setting his hands on her hips.

"He's a kid," Maurie said, moving her hands on his shoulders. "And he's sweet."

Grant held her gaze. "I'm glad you think so." He slid his hands behind her back, drawing her even closer. "I think you're sweet too."

Maurie tilted her head. "Thanks for dinner."

"You're welcome," he said with a slow smile. "Thanks for coming, and for being patient with a four-year old. Not the ideal Valentine's date, I know."

Maurie lifted a shoulder. "I didn't mind."

Grant lowered his head and kissed the edge of her jaw. "Hopefully Trent will go right to sleep, because I've been waiting all night to do this." He kissed her on the lips then.

His mouth was warm, and the scruff of his chin tickled hers. Maurie felt all melty inside as his hands moved up her back. She breathed him in and sighed. She so wanted to get lost, but she'd also seen his distress earlier.

"Grant," she said, pulling away.

He opened his eyes, and slowly his gaze focused.

"What was the phone call about at the restaurant?" she asked, before she could be tempted to kiss him again.

Grant lifted a hand and moved his fingers along her shoulder. "I don't really want to talk about it."

"Because it was about me?" she asked.

Grant's hand stilled. "Yes, but it doesn't matter."

"I think it does matter," Maurie said. "You were pretty upset."

Grant released a sigh. "Joy was being . . . Joy."

Maurie waited.

"Okay." Grant moved his hands to her waist, holding her loosely in his arms. "She did some googling on you and found out about your mom."

This Maurie hadn't expected, but maybe she shouldn't be surprised. It would have come up eventually—if she and Grant continued in their relationship.

"Joy is a paranoid person, and very controlling, as you know," he continued. "She panicked and said some unfair things."

"About my mom?"

"What she said about your mom was true, but she extended them to you."

"Oh." Maurie drew away from Grant, but he grasped her hand before she could step away completely.

"Maurie, I don't want you to worry about Joy," Grant said. "She has an acid tongue. And she doesn't like it when she thinks other people might have things better than she does."

Maurie frowned and looked down at Grant's hand holding hers. "Like what? She seems pretty well settled. She has Stone, and Trent too."

"Joy will never be truly happy," Grant said. "I've had to accept that. She'll criticize any woman I choose to date." He squeezed her hand. "But I'm not going to let her criticize you, Maurie. You're too important to me."

She swallowed against the tightness in her throat. He'd defended her against his ex-wife. That had to be significant, right?

"I wish Joy were a better person," he continued. "But the fact is that I'll always have to deal with her because of Trent. And I don't want you to have to worry about her."

Maurie took a deep breath, then met Grant's gaze head-on. "Don't shut me out, Grant. Even if it has to do with Joy. Because if we're going to be in a relationship . . . or whatever is going on between us . . . I need to be a part of all of it. The good, the bad, and the ugly."

Grant gazed at her for a long moment. "Is that what you want? To be in a relationship with me?"

Maurie's face heated. "Only if you want it too."

One edge of his mouth lifted. "I'll make you a deal."

She stared at him, not sure where he was going with this.

"Dance with me, and it will be the official start of our relationship," he said in a low voice. "I think it will help me forget about that phone call with Joy."

Twenty-Two

Maurie didn't look exactly pleased that he'd brought up dancing again.

"What's wrong?" he asked, not breaking his gaze.

"I've never danced before," she said, then looked away.

Grant stared at her. She'd been homeschooled, yes, then moved, but surely . . . Now he felt like an idiot. "Is it too late to learn?"

Her eyes met his again, and he didn't like the sadness he saw in them.

"I don't think I'd be any good at it," she said. "Plus there's no music, and my shoes—"

Grant released her and pulled his cell phone out of his pocket. He turned it on, then opened a music app.

"Trent will wake up," Maurie said.

"Believe me, he sleeps like a rock." Grant started the music, then set the phone on the counter.

Maurie placed her hands on her hips. "I'm not going to dance with you in a kitchen."

Grant chuckled. "Why not? No one's here to see you if you trip."

Her cheeks stained red, which only made her look more beautiful.

He bent down and grasped her ankle.

"What are you doing?" she protested, her eyes flashing.

"Taking off your shoes." He lifted her foot and undid the very small strap. He wondered if the shoe manufacturers purposely made the buckles on these things tiny. Then he set the shoe aside and reached for her other foot.

Miraculously, Maurie let him take off her other shoe.

He straightened and smiled. The music that was playing was a slow beat. "It's not hard," he said. "Just move with me."

Maurie exhaled, as if she'd given up arguing with him. Grant counted that as a win.

He took her hands and set one on his shoulder, then he clasped her other hand in his. Next, he drew her close. She stepped easily into his arms, and he relished the feel of her warm, soft body against his.

"Just follow my lead," he whispered. He swayed to the music for a moment, and when he felt Maurie relaxing, he took a step and began to turn in a slow circle.

"See, it's not that hard, is it?" he asked.

"We're hardly moving," Maurie whispered.

"That's okay." Grant drew away slightly to meet her gaze. "There aren't really any rules here."

Her eyes had softened. "This is rather nice. I didn't know you were such a romantic."

"I don't know if I'd go that far," he said.

"Flowers yesterday," she said. "Dancing today. What's next?"

Grant chuckled and drew her close again. He rested his cheek next to hers, and her breathing quickened. "Every day's a new adventure with you." And it was.

"Glad you think so," Maurie said in a quiet tone.

Fortunately Trent stayed in his room, asleep, and Grant was able to dance several songs with Maurie. In the kitchen of all places. He couldn't think of a better place.

"So . . . I should go," Maurie said. "I have to play catch-up on some things."

He didn't want to let her go, but Trent would be up early. Although it wasn't like Grant ever really slept in anyway. He released Maurie, but kept hold of one hand. "I'm sorry again about Joy, and about Trent monopolizing you."

"Stop apologizing," Maurie said with a half smile. "My life is no piece of cake either."

"That's why I don't want to make it harder," Grant said, linking their fingers.

"You're not." Maurie lifted up on her toes and kissed his cheek. "You're making my life better, Grant Shelton," she said next to his ear.

Grant exhaled, and before she could pull away, he cradled her face with both hands and kissed her. It seemed the more he was around her, the more he wanted her around. He knew it was getting late, but he didn't want her to go.

Maurie twined her arms about his neck, pressed against him, and kissed him back.

When they broke apart to breathe, Grant said, "Stay. We can watch a movie, then tomorrow live on caffeine."

Maurie kissed him again, this one was more of a quick, goodbye peck. "You're very tempting. But that's exactly the problem . . . You're very tempting."

He gazed into her green eyes. "I could say the same about you."

"Hmm." Maurie lowered her arms and stepped back.

Grant leaned against the counter and watched her reach for her shoes. "Do you want me to put those on for you?"

Maurie smirked. "No, thank you. I think you're just stalling."

He chuckled. "I'm definitely stalling."

She slipped on her shoes and buckled the straps. "See you sometime."

Grant walked her outside to her car. "We'll come by the shop tomorrow, because I'm sure that Trent will be talking about you nonstop."

"Okay," she said, turning when she reached the driver's side of her car.

The cold air was biting, but he didn't mind. "And I'll be thinking about you nonstop,"

The smile on her face was what he wanted to see.

"I'll see you tomorrow then," she said, her breath a cloud.

"Bye." Grant didn't move. Neither did she.

"It's cold," she said at last.

"Very cold," he agreed.

Maurie threw her arms about his neck, and he pulled her close. He breathed her in.

When Maurie left, Grant went back into his apartment and sat at the kitchen table, replaying everything about the evening in his mind. Trent was definitely attached to Maurie, and Grant knew that he was too. He just had to figure out a way to keep Joy from getting in the middle of things. Or saying something to Trent that he might inadvertently repeat to Maurie.

Grant scrubbed a hand through his hair, hating that Joy could be so cruel. At least Maurie had seemed to take it all in stride and had stayed to dance with him. He smiled at the thought. Thinking about her only made him miss her, and she'd only been gone a short time. Then he frowned at how she'd never danced before now. Her childhood had been rough, and he probably didn't even know the whole of it. Yet she was resilient. Grant was glad Maurie had gone into a good foster home at least.

After Joy's tirade, he felt more protective of Maurie than ever.

He picked up his phone and sent her a text: *Did you get home okay?*

Yes, she texted back. *Are you watching a movie without me?*

He smiled and wrote, *No way. You took the party with you.*

A minute later her reply came. *I like you, Grant Shelton.*

I more than like you, he wrote. It might be a bit too forward, but it was the truth.

You're definitely a romantic, she texted.

Only around you, it seems.

Maurie sent a heart-eye emoji.

Grant decided that it was going to be a long night. He'd be surprised if he slept at all.

It turned out that he did sleep, and for longer than usual. Trent climbed into his bed at 8:30 a.m. and yep, asked where Maurie was.

Grant tousled his son's hair. "Maurie's working at her new store. Remember we went there Friday?"

"Can we go again?" Trent asked. "I want more donuts."

"I don't think they have donuts again," Grant said. "But maybe we can take her a treat later. We should go visit Grandma and Grandpa. Remember they want to see you?"

Trent's expression brightened. "Yeah!"

Grant chuckled. "Make your bed, and I'll get breakfast ready."

Trent scrambled off the bed and sped out of the room, which made Grant laugh. Then suddenly Trent was back. "Can you make scrabbled eggs?"

"Sure thing." Grant climbed out of bed and went into the kitchen. The sight of it reminded him of dancing with Maurie last night. He wondered if it was too early to text her.

So he returned to his room and unplugged his phone from his charger. He sat on the edge of his bed and wrote: *Good morning.*

She wrote back a few seconds later. *Good morning.*

Grant smiled, and he texted her again.

That's how Trent found him a few minutes later. "Where's the scrabbled eggs?" he asked.

Grant looked up. "Oh, sorry. I'm on it right now, buddy."

"Can I play on your phone?" Trent asked, following him to the kitchen.

"Um, no, but you can pick a cartoon after breakfast while I'm in the shower." He set his phone on top of the fridge. Then he opened the door and pulled out the carton of eggs.

Trent climbed up on a kitchen chair and continued to pepper Grant with questions as he fixed breakfast.

For the first time, Grant thought that Trent needed a sibling. Someone to play with. The thought gave him pause. Even if Grant were to have another kid, the kid would be several years younger. Not exactly a playmate.

Grant shook the thought away. His mind was doing all kinds of twisty things.

His phone chimed from on top of the fridge, and he picked it up. Maurie had replied to his latest text. Grant chuckled.

"What's funny, Daddy?" Trent asked.

Grant set the phone back on the fridge. "Nothing. Can you get spoons out for us?" He didn't want Trent starting in with the questions about Maurie again. Grant grabbed a couple of bowls from the cupboard, then he scooped the scrambled eggs into the bowls.

Trent had found his seat again with two spoons in hand. Grant set the bowls on the table, then he took a seat.

After they finished eating, Trent sat on the couch,

watching cartoons. Grant jumped in the shower. When he got out, instead of texts from Maurie, there was a text from Joy. With a sigh, he opened it and read.

What he read made him feel like he'd been punched in the gut. Joy wasn't going to relent.

I called your parents this morning and asked them about your girlfriend. They didn't even know you're dating. So strange. Because you're hiding something? Anyway, when I told them who you were dating, they were shocked. Your mom also confirmed that Maurie lived in a druggie house. Grant, we're not done talking about this. Either we come to an agreement, or I call my lawyer.

Grant gritted his teeth and read through the text a second time. Just then, his phone rang. His dad was calling. Which meant that his mother was upset. Rarely did his dad call; mostly it was his mom.

"Hi, Dad," Grant said.

"Joy called us and—"

"I know," Grant said. "Trent and I are coming over in about twenty minutes. We can talk then."

His dad paused. "Okay... Is everything all right?"

"Mostly," Grant said. "I'll see you soon, and tell Mom not to worry." He hung up before his dad could ask any more questions.

Grant didn't reply to Joy. He'd make her wait until after he did damage control with his parents. Crossing to his closet, he pulled out a long-sleeved shirt, then dug out jeans from his dresser drawer. He was annoyed, and he hated that Joy was infiltrating his weekend with their son. In fact... he might as well kill two birds with one stone. He texted his sister, Julie: *Heading over to Mom and Dad's this morning. If you can come over too, that would be great. I need to talk to the family about something important.*

Julie wrote back almost immediately. *Do you have cancer?*

No, Grant texted. *It's about Maurie, if you must know.*

Is she pregnant?

Grant scoffed. *No, again. Come over, and you can ask your questions then. Oh, and Trent's with me, so bring Riley.*

How did you end up with Trent this weekend? Julie wrote.

Grant ignored that text too. He'd never get out of his house with all this texting, and he could explain everything in person. He left his bedroom and found Trent still on the couch. "Get dressed, buddy, then we'll go. Grandma and Grandpa are waiting for us."

The drive to his parents' new retirement condo took less than ten minutes. The short distance only made Grant feel guilty that he didn't see his parents much. His mother's constant efforts at trying to set him up on blind dates had put a strain between them. So now she should be pretty happy he was dating someone, right?

Despite Trent's peppy chatter, Grant couldn't shake the moodiness that had come over him. He shouldn't let Joy affect his moods so much. They'd been divorced for years. Yet she'd gone below the belt with dragging his parents into their argument.

Trent had unbuckled his seatbelt by the time Grant parked the SUV.

Grant turned. "What did I tell you about keeping your seatbelt on until I turn off the car?" His voice was probably sharper than needed.

Trent's chin jutted out, and Grant knew he had to ease off or he might have a crying kid.

"Sorry," Trent said. "Should I put it back on?"

"No." Grant sighed. "It's too late now. I want you to be safe, okay?"

"Okay."

Grant climbed out of the car, and within a few minutes they were inside his parents' place and enveloped in floral-scented hugs from his mom. His mother was a petite woman, formerly blonde and now gray since she'd fully embraced her gray hair and kept it short and spikey.

His dad was the tall one, and Grant had inherited that height.

"Good to see you, son," his dad said, and they gave each other a quick hug and pat on the back.

Tension came from both of his parents, but they were acting cheerful for Trent's sake.

"Julie's coming over too," Grant said.

His parents exchanged significant looks, and Grant tried not to let that bother him. He'd be the one calling the shots this morning.

"Is she bringing Riley?" Trent asked.

"Yep," Grant said, and hoped it was the case. In the next moment, someone knocked.

His mom opened it, and Julie walked in with Riley. After more greetings were over, his mom said, "Hey, boys, I have puzzles set up in Grandpa's office. I'll bring in some snacks too."

The boys cheered and ran down the hall.

"Let's sit in the living room," his dad said.

Grant took a seat on one of the wingback chairs. Julie sat in the other one, and his parents sat close together on the couch as if they needed support from each other.

Everyone seemed to be waiting for him to start, so Grant said, "I hope you can erase everything from your mind that Joy told you. She's only right about one thing. I am dating Maurie Ledbetter."

Julie smiled. "I knew it!"

But his parents shared no such enthusiasm.

"I don't understand," his mother said. "The Ledbetters were... Well, Joy has a right to be concerned. *I'm* concerned."

"Maurie is nothing like her mother, if that's what you're worried about," Grant said. "Joy has issues with *me* moving on, although she can move on all she likes. Maurie returned to Pine Valley a few weeks ago and opened the new Every Occasion shop."

His mother's furrowed brow relaxed. "That's *Maurie's* place?"

"Yes," Grant said, and he went on to give them a brief history of what Maurie had done since leaving Pine Valley. Then he finished with, "Before you pass judgment, I want you to meet her."

Twenty-Three

"He invited me over to his *parents'* for dinner," Maurie told Taffy.

Taffy looked up from the display she was organizing in their shop.

Business had been brisk in the morning, but around three they'd hit a dead spot. No one was in the store right now, and Grant had just texted Maurie that he wanted her to come with him to his parents' that night... for dinner.

Taffy quirked an eyebrow. "Wow, really?"

Maurie exhaled and leaned on the counter next to the cash register. "Grant's family knows me as the teenager with a druggie mom."

Taffy set down the basket she was holding and crossed to Maurie. "You *were* the teenager with a druggie mom. It's part of your past, and it's also part of why you're so strong and amazing now."

"I don't feel strong *or* amazing," Maurie said.

"Oh, hon." Taffy stepped forward and hugged her. "Believe me, you are. If you weren't, I wouldn't be out here in this small town stuffing baskets."

Maurie gave a soft laugh. "You'd be in London living it up?"

Taffy drew away and grinned. "Something like that." She settled her hands on her hips. "Grant's parents will love you. If they're half as great as Grant, then you have nothing to worry about."

"So you like him, huh?"

Taffy was still smiling. "Let's just say that if you dumped him, I'd get in line. Although he pretty much already told me there's no future between us."

"What?" Maurie stared at her friend.

Taffy told her about her first meeting with Grant.

"I had no idea." Maurie shook her head. "Maybe you could come with me. Be the backup friend. Give me support."

"Um, no," Taffy said. "I have other plans tonight."

Maurie's brows shot up. "Oh? Netflix?"

Taffy's cheeks pinked, and Maurie wondered if she'd *ever* seen Taffy blush.

"I might have a date," Taffy said. "But that's all you're getting out of me for now."

Maurie scoffed. "I tell you everything, Taffy, and you're holding back on me now."

Taffy grinned and turned away. "Let's just say that Pine Valley is starting to grow on me." She busied herself with the table arrangement again. "But seriously, Maurie, just be your amazing self. I don't doubt that by the end of tonight you'll have Grant's parents in love with you too."

"What do you mean by 'too'?" Maurie asked.

Taffy glanced over at her. "You know what I'm talking about, girl. Even you can't deny that Grant is head over heels for you."

The breath left Maurie. The thought that Grant could be in love with her was staggering... especially because she knew she was in love with him. "How can you be sure?"

Taffy shrugged. "One of my gifts, I guess." She waved a hand. "Now text the man back. Don't leave him hanging. He took a giant leap forward in your relationship."

Maurie swallowed. Taffy was right. This was a major step—meeting Grant's parents. Was she ready for it? She wanted to meet them, and she was more than happy that Grant had asked. But would they ask about her mom? Would they worry too about their grandson, just as Joy had?

Maurie opened Grant's text and replied: *Sounds good. What time should I be ready?*

Grant wrote back a minute later: *We'll pick you up at 5:30.*

"We" because it would include Trent too, which might actually help things, Maurie decided.

The rest of the afternoon went by too quickly, probably because Maurie was getting more and more nervous about the evening. She'd met Brandon's parents once at a giant party that he'd thrown. They'd been introduced, and they had chatted for a few minutes, but that was about it.

So after work Maurie found herself changing into a fresh outfit while Taffy was in the shower getting ready for her mystery date. Maurie chose to dress a little nicer than casual since she didn't want to look like the homeless waif she'd been when Grant's parents last saw her. She wore black slacks and a cream sweater, then decided to add a black-and-blue scarf too. She twisted her hair up and used a decorative clip, hoping it would make her look more sophisticated.

When the doorbell rang, Maurie nearly jumped. It *was* five thirty. She opened the door to find only Grant on the porch. He was wearing a light shirt and black leather jacket, complete with faded jeans and loafers with no socks.

"Aren't your feet cold?" she asked, because apparently that was the best greeting she could come up with.

"Not really," Grant said, his blue eyes scanning her.

Maurie didn't miss the appreciation in his gaze, and the butterflies in her stomach beat faster. Pretty much every kiss they'd shared the night before came flooding back to her mind. Wow, she was nervous. "Where's Trent?" she asked.

"At my parents'," Grant said, lifting a brow. "I told Joy I'd be bringing Trent home tomorrow. Missing a day of preschool isn't going to kill him." He reached for her hand, and she realized she'd been hovering in the doorway, stalling.

She stepped onto the porch, and Grant kept pulling her toward him until she was flush against him.

"Hi," he whispered.

She met his gaze. "Hi."

"Nervous?"

She swallowed. "Very."

He didn't laugh, which was good. Instead, he lifted his other hand and brushed his thumb along her cheek. Then he lowered his head and kissed her. It was slow, yet light, and Maurie sighed into him. She felt herself relaxing little by little.

Grant smiled against her mouth. "Better?"

She breathed. "I think so. Maybe you should do that again."

So he did. Maurie was dimly aware that anyone driving by would be a witness to her standing on the porch kissing Grant. But she didn't hear any passing cars, at least that she knew of.

When Grant drew away, Maurie did feel better. The knots in her stomach had eased, and she felt steadier just being with Grant.

"So, don't be surprised if my parents know quite a bit about you," Grant said. "Between me and Trent, they've heard a lot."

This didn't help Maurie's nerves. "Is that good?"

Grant led her down the porch steps, and they walked to his SUV. "It's all good. They're excited that you're coming over." He opened the passenger door for her, and she climbed into the warm SUV.

It was kind of strange being in the car without Trent and his chatter coming from the back seat.

Grant climbed in, and the drive to his parents' condo sped by as he told her what Trent had been up to that day. Maurie laughed at the stories, and her heart softened even more toward the little guy.

When Grant parked in the parking lot of the condo complex, he turned to her. "I need to tell you something. But I don't want you to worry over it."

He told her how Joy had called his parents and brought up her concerns over Maurie's upbringing. "I was furious, to say the least," Grant said. "So this morning I met with my parents and explained everything—about you—and about *us*. They know how I feel about you, Maurie, and they know that Joy can be overdramatic."

Maurie focused on the "how I feel about you" comment. How *did* Grant feel about her? Was he in love with her, as Taffy had said?

"So they don't have the same concerns as Joy?" Maurie said.

"Not after I talked to them," Grant assured her. He reached for her hand. "Julie and her husband will be here too."

"Kill all the birds with one stone?" Maurie said.

"Something like that," Grant said. "Are you okay with this?"

She held his gaze. "I'm okay with it. I'm still nervous though."

Grant brought her hand to his mouth and pressed a kiss on the back of it. "I'm nervous too, but not for the same reason."

Before Maurie could ask him what he meant, he released her hand and opened his door. In mere seconds, she'd be meeting his family. She could do this. Be normal, cheerful, friendly, and hopefully his family would look beyond her past.

Grant opened her door, and as they walked to his parents' place, he took hold of her hand again. He rang the doorbell, and soon the door opened.

A dark-haired woman stood there, one who had similar features to Grant, but more feminine.

"I wanted to greet you first," the woman said. "I'm Julie, Grant's sister."

"Hi," Maurie said, and she stuck out her hand to shake. But Julie drew her into a hug. "We hug in the Shelton family. Come in. I hope my brother's treating you well."

"Uh—"

"Come on, my mom's in the kitchen," Julie continued.

Grant leaned close to Maurie. "My sister's a talker; did I warn you?"

"I heard that," Julie said with a smirk.

And just like that, Maurie was separated from Grant, because Julie had a hold of her arm and was leading her toward the kitchen.

"Maurie!" Trent said from where he was perched on a barstool at a long counter. Next to him was another young kid, who must be the cousin. A little girl about two year old sat in a high chair.

Trent slipped off the barstool and ran toward Maurie. He barreled into her legs, and Maurie was lucky to stay upright and hug him back. She laughed, then looked up to see an older woman watching them. Grant's mother. Her eyes were kind, and her mouth curved upward. She had the same-colored eyes as Grant.

"Hello," Maurie said.

"Welcome," Mrs. Shelton said, her tone a bit formal.

"Easy, buddy," Grant said to Trent, coming into the kitchen. "What did I say about running into people?"

Maurie straightened and met Grant's gaze. "It's okay. I'm stronger than I look."

"Yeah, Daddy, she's super strong."

"I guess I'm outvoted then," Grant said, slipping his arm around her waist.

In front of his mother, no less.

"Mom, this is Maurie," he said. "I don't think you've officially met before."

Mrs. Shelton smiled and wiped her hands on her apron. The counter behind her had flour and dough on it. "It's nice to officially meet you."

"You too," Maurie said, taking courage from Grant's arm around her waist. "What are you making?"

"Oh, this is dessert," Mrs. Shelton said.

"Donuts!" Trent proclaimed. "We get to watch them bubble."

Mrs. Shelton smiled at her grandson, then turned her gaze back to Maurie. "I just need to get them fried up, then we'll have dinner."

"I can help," Maurie said, deciding that she might as well jump in with both feet.

"You don't have to," Grant murmured, but Maurie had already stepped away from his touch.

She walked to the counter. "You made them into balls?"

"Yes," Mrs. Shelton said. "Do you like to cook?"

"I love to," Maurie said. "It's like therapy to me. My foster mom was a gourmet cook, and she pretty much taught me everything."

Mrs. Shelton was silent for a moment.

Maurie hoped that she hadn't said something to make the

woman uncomfortable. But if anything between Maurie and Grant were going to truly work, she wouldn't be quiet about her past.

"Well, that's lovely," Mrs. Shelton said at last, and her tone was much warmer. "Have you made donuts before?"

"Once, but it's been years," Maurie said. "I've made scones, though, and it's not much different, right?"

"Right," Mrs. Shelton confirmed. "If you could roll the last of the balls, then I'll get the first batch into the fryer."

Maurie moved to the sink and washed her hands. Within moments, she and Mrs. Shelton had a sort of assembly line going. Maurie rolled dough, and Grant's mom fried them up. Julie joined in and arranged the fried donuts on a platter, then sprinkled them with powdered sugar.

At one point, Grant brought his father into the kitchen and introduced them. Maurie could see where Grant got his height and build from, and she was pleased that Mr. Shelton was open and friendly right from the start.

Mrs. Shelton was also warming up with each passing minute. It seemed that cooking and food could bond all types of women.

When the donuts were finished and left to cool off in the kitchen, Maurie walked with Mrs. Shelton into the dining room. The table had been beautifully set, and the sight of it brought a wave of nostalgia. It reminded her so much of what her foster mom might have done.

The dinner went smoothly—in fact, better than Maurie expected. Both of Grant's parents asked her a few questions, and Julie was chatty the whole time. Her husband seemed like a pleasant guy—quiet but attentive.

The homemade donuts were definitely a highlight of the evening, and Maurie laughed more than once watching Trent and Riley's enthusiasm. What would it be like to be kids with such loving families? Maurie would never know, but she was grateful to be a part of this evening. The love between the family members was tangible.

When Julie said she had to get Riley home to bed, and Grant concurred that he had to get Trent home as well, Maurie was surprised how fast the time had gone.

"We need to help clean up," Maurie said.

Mrs. Shelton quickly cut in. "Maybe next time. You two are off the hook tonight."

"If you're sure," Maurie said.

"I'm sure," Mrs. Shelton said. She stepped forward and enveloped Maurie into a hug. "It was lovely to meet you, and thank you for coming."

Maurie didn't know why the woman's words made her feel like crying. She blinked against the stinging in her eyes.

Goodbyes were fairly chaotic, as Julie's family was leaving at the same time.

As they walked out together, Trent hopped ahead, chattering with Riley. It sounded like they were making playdate plans for the next day. Grant took her hand, linking their fingers together.

"Hey, Grant," Julie said. "Can Trent sleep over tonight? Riley has been begging me."

Maurie could feel Grant's hesitation, but then he said, "Okay, that's fine."

Ahead of them, the boys cheered.

Maurie laughed and squeezed Grant's hand, just before Trent ran up to the both of them. He hugged his dad, then he hugged Maurie.

The boys followed after Julie's husband to their car, and Julie turned to Maurie. "My parents were very impressed with you, I could tell. And don't let anything Joy says bother you. Grant told us all about it. Just know that you're ten times better than Joy ever was, and you have all of our full approval."

"Maurie doesn't need anyone's approval," Grant cut in.

Julie held up her hand to stop her brother. "Even so, you'd better treat this woman right, because she's the best thing that ever happened to you, Grant."

Maurie decided she really liked Julie.

"As for you, Maurie," Julie said. "Keep doing what you're doing. You're perfect." She stepped forward and hugged Maurie.

Maurie didn't think she'd ever been hugged so much in her life.

After Julie and her family left with Trent, Grant grasped Maurie's hand, and they walked to his SUV.

When they reached the passenger's side door, he turned to Maurie. "Julie's right. My parents loved you."

Maurie let those words buzz through her. "They're pretty amazing. Your mom reminds me a lot of my foster mom, Gladys. Not only does your mom love to cook, but she was so accepting."

"You're not a hard person to accept," Grant said, a smile turning up the corners of his mouth. He leaned closer to her and put his hand on the SUV behind her, so that she was between him and the SUV.

"So . . . it looks like we have the rest of the evening to ourselves," he said in a low tone.

Maurie met his eyes, and she felt the intensity of his gaze burning through her. "Whatever will we do by ourselves?" she teased.

Grant moved a few inches closer. "I could think of a few things."

Maurie arched her brows. "Like what?" she asked in a soft voice.

He closed the distance and kissed her. She slipped her arms around his neck and pulled him in. Closing her eyes, she kissed him back. Her heart was beating erratically. His mouth explored hers for a long moment.

When he drew away, he held her gaze, and she realized that she didn't feel a bit of the cold night.

"Remember when I told you I was nervous too, but not about my parents?" he whispered.

"Mm-hm." It was a distant memory, since his kisses made everything else distant.

"I need to tell you something, Maurie Ledbetter."

This brought her out of her haze, and she drew back enough to meet his eyes. The intensity in his gaze made her pulse skyrocket.

"I'm in love with you, Maurie," he said. "When I first saw you after so many years, all I knew was that whatever had happened in each of our lives, I wanted to begin again with you."

Maurie stared at him, this man who had watched over her when she was a lost girl in a lost life. A man who was still watching over her. The warmth from his gaze was heating her all over . . . and the love in his eyes she hoped to never see disappear. Because she knew without a doubt that she felt the same way. "I love you too, Grant Shelton. And I agree. Let's begin again."

Grant cradled her face with his hands, and then he kissed her again. This time, the kissing wasn't slow and warm. It was more fiery, more passionate, more encompassing, and she decided they probably needed to leave the parking lot.

When Grant drew away, he whispered against her mouth, "Do you want to dance?"

It took a minute for her mind to focus. "Out here?"

"I was thinking we could find a kitchen somewhere," he said, amusement in his tone.

Maurie smiled, then she laughed. Grant Shelton was one

of a kind, and there was no other man she'd rather be with, and no other place she'd rather live than right here in Pine Valley. "Your kitchen or mine?"

Want to read more stories set in Pine Valley?

Want to read about the realtor Jeff Finch? Check out WORTH THE RISK

What about Gwen from the restaurant? Read WAITING FOR YOU

Will Felicity at the bookshop get a Happily Ever After? Read FINDING US

Heather B. Moore is a four-time *USA Today* bestselling author. She writes historical thrillers under the pen name H.B. Moore; her latest thrillers include *The Killing Curse* and *Breaking Jess*. Under the name Heather B. Moore, she writes romance and women's fiction. Her newest releases include the historical romances *Love is Come* and *Ruth*. She's also one of the coauthors of the *USA Today* bestselling series: A Timeless Romance Anthology. Heather writes speculative fiction under the pen name Jane Redd; releases include the Solstice series and *Mistress Grim*. Heather is represented by Dystel, Goderich & Bourret.

For book updates, sign up for Heather's email list: hbmoore.com/contact
Website: HBMoore.com
Facebook: Fans of H. B. Moore
Blog: MyWritersLair.blogspot.com
Instagram: @authorhbmoore
Twitter: @HeatherBMoore

www.ingramcontent.com/pod-product-compliance
Lightning Source LLC
LaVergne TN
LVHW021814060526
838201LV00058B/3373